THE DSA SEASON TWO, BOOK TWO

FOUNDATIONS

Also by Lou Paduano

The Greystone Saga

Signs of Portents

Tales from Portents

The Medusa Coin

Pathways in the Dark

A Circle of Shadows

Greystone-in-Training

Hammer and Anvil

The Gifts of Kali

The Final Gauntlet

The DSA

Season One

The Clearing

Promethean

The Bridge

Spectral Advocate

Dark Impulses

Broken Loyalties

Season Two

The Wellspring

THE DSA SEASON TWO, BOOK TWO

FOUNDATIONS

Lou Paduano

Eleven Ten Publishing LLC

GRAND ISLAND, NEW YORK

Eleven Ten Publishing LLC
282 Fareway Lane
Grand Island, NY 14072

Printed in the United States of America
Edited by JP Services.
Cover art design by MiblArt

First edition published 2023

Library of Congress Cataloguing in Publication Data
Paduano, Lou
Foundations / Lou Paduano

LCCN: 2023918949
ISBN-13: 978-1-944965-39-6 (paperback)
ISBN-13: 978-1-944965-38-9 (eBook)

For Paul

CHAPTER ONE

Percival Jenkins wondered when life got away from him. It hadn't been an overnight affair. Somewhere along the way, amid business loans, payroll insurance, and a dozen other tasks that ate at the free time he had once spent binge-watching the same movies repeatedly on cable, the man of twenty-nine simply lost track of what life was supposed to be about.

In the years since opening Bethesda Swag, Percival's top priorities shifted from fulfilling the dreams of his youth to turning a profit. He was the envy of the guys at the monthly Chamber of Commerce meetings, yet lacked any genuine connections in his life.

He missed the simplicity of his youth. Hell, he missed a day off once a week—a rarity he could ill-afford for fear of some calamity striking the store.

Thankfully, today passed without incident. Twelve hours had amounted to less than ten patrons browsing the shelves. Only three had made a purchase—two of which were supposed "gag" gifts for friends. He expected to see the shirts hanging in the window of the local Goodwill in a few months.

The lock slid into place. He held the key for a long moment to test the mechanism. The handle shook under his grip, but the door remained in place. It was his nightly ritual, one that soothed him, yet irritated him at the same time.

"Okay," he muttered through his routine. "The drawer is locked up in the safe. Receipts counted. That took a long time. Pfftt. Let's see, what else?"

He put the store's operation on his shoulders. Most of his colleagues spoke of managers carrying the load while they hit the links for a quick nine, or whatever people say when they play golf between beers. Percival never trusted in anyone that much—not with his store, and definitely not with his livelihood.

"Have to remember to have Sue stay for inventory next week," Percival said. "Or is it Jasper's turn? I should write it down. Why don't I write more down?"

He turned from the store, then stopped. A quick shift and his hand was back at the handle. Three shakes reminded Percival that the lock remained in place.

"See you tomorrow morning, beautiful. Bright and early."

He cursed the schedule. He condemned the never-ending pull the store maintained in every decision he made—or didn't—in his life. Still, the store was his, and he took pride in that despite the nightmare it caused on a personal level.

"It could always be worse," he grumbled. His hands shot into the pockets of his tan trench coat. He left the safety of the awning over the store, and the rain greeted him for the walk home.

Lightning struck behind him. The sound made him jump, and the intensity drove him deeper into the rain. Wind swept the street. Loose paper and trash swirled about him. Percival tucked his head lower to push through the growing storm.

He turned at the sound of more lightning. His eyes widened at the sight of purple bolts slamming along the pavement. They formed above the rooftops, not from the clouds in the black sky. Each strike concentrated on a single area, one of the converted warehouses across the street that now served as a fitness center.

"What the hell?"

The lightning spun, no longer content with hitting the ground. The purple beams coalesced into an oval-shaped hole in the middle of the air, just off the ground.

As the portal grew, a figure formed at its center. He fell through the hole in space to the pavement, landing on hands and knees. Purple energy sizzled as it streamed off the newcomer.

With its occupant discharged, the portal shrank. Light flashed, blinding Percival. When he opened his eyes again to the street, the hole was gone and only the man remained.

"H-H-Hey," Percival stammered, working up his nerve. Part of him wanted to return to the locked door of his store to start his routine over. The other half screamed to run like hell. His feet, however, stuck to the pavement. "Are you all right? Do you need me to call someone for help?"

The man stood; he towered over Percival's five-and-a-half-foot frame. His clothes, what appeared to be a military uniform of some kind, stuck to his skin. The man's bones were visible in multiple areas, like he hadn't had a meal in years. Gaunt didn't do him justice. Around his neck, he wore a collar with blue lights adorning the unique accessory.

"I have a phone you can use if you—"

Percival's offer ended the second the man's eyes opened. Percival saw no pupils, only a deep red—like they were drowning in blood.

"Oh, God."

Percival ran. His body still worked well enough to recognize danger, and he let his survival instinct take over. He flew down Elm, then turned left on Arlington for uptown. Percival crossed busy intersections; cars beeped their dismay at his stupidity. He didn't care. All that mattered was getting away from the man with the red eyes.

Three blocks passed before Percival could do no more, and he stopped at the corner. He hugged tight to the lamppost. The rain pounded harder than ever. Three teenagers threw him queer looks, then giggled as they continued to the bar across the street. Others stared at his actions while they murmured to their friends.

The man from the glowing portal was nowhere to be seen.

Percival let out a deep breath. "Probably just a loon. Hopped up on something."

The rationale was enough to calm Percival's nerves for a second. He turned from the lights of the street and started back toward home.

At the end of the block, a hand shot out and snatched his coat. Percival's feet left the ground as the darkness between buildings swallowed him whole. Red eyes loomed over him.

"Please," Percival said. His hands clasped before him, unable to act against the towering menace. "I didn't see anything. I didn't do anything."

People passed the alley without a look. He tried to call out to them, but his words caught in his throat. The man with the red eyes grabbed him by the neck and hoisted him against the wall.

When the people cut across the street to meet their friends, the man dropped Percival to the ground.

The wounded fool rubbed his neck. "Why? Why me?"

A low growl escaped the man's lips.

"You don't have to do this," Percival said. "You don't have to—"

Percival's attacker opened his mouth. Razor sharp fangs greeted the terrified shopkeeper. There wasn't even time for him to scream before the end arrived.

The body dropped to the concrete, and the hunter gave a satisfied roar.

Through fire and storm, over the shrill screams of hell itself, he had returned to the world. Much had changed somehow. Moving away from his victim, the sensations hit him all at once. The smell of the place seemed different; the air was even more diluted than he recalled from his first trip through the portal.

His victim, though, had been waiting for him. His target had stood in the rain and greeted him, as if unable to recognize the threat before him.

The chase had done nothing to sway him, the pleading little more than an irritant. Nothing would stop the hunter from achieving his goal.

His target's broken and bleeding body lay on the cracked concrete. His cries ended before any disruption had occurred. There had been no need to draw in more victims. Only the one had been given as the mission.

The hunter surveyed his dead prey, sniffing the air. Another anomaly caught in his nostrils. He reached for the body to turn it over. Everything appeared to be correct. The man's height was average, the same in build. The tan coat matched the one he remembered. Even the mussed up hair from a long day and the tired eyes matched as well.

Yet the man carried no weapon like before. The hunter clawed at the man's coat in his search. There was no identification, no license or badge to fit into his pockets. He found nothing, except an over-sized ring filled with jingling keys and grocery store membership cards.

The hunter growled in frustration. He couldn't be wrong. After struggling to make it back, after being lost in the ether, he couldn't let his mission end in failure.

The evidence before his very eyes told a different tale. The victim at his feet was nothing more than a mistake.

There could be no more.

The hunter slipped into the shadows of night. The hunt was on, and it was only a matter of time before he found his true target.

CHAPTER TWO

Wesley Fuller gripped the television remote like it was a life-sustaining IV. He kept it tucked close, unwilling to let the others in the room so much as look at it, let alone steal it from him. He was enjoying yet another *Law & Order* marathon. The show comforted him. It kept his mind moving.

No one else in the common room of the Happy Acres Retirement Village cared for it. They always preferred something happier, something from their youth that made them smile rather than the murder spree that typically accompanied Wesley's picks.

While most stayed quiet, suffering in silence over Wesley's power grab with the remote, some turned their attention to other diversions. There were games to play, cards being the most popular choice with the senior crowd. Some slept through the entire ordeal. A select few made their wishes clear and threw nasty glares at him as they shuffled past.

Wesley paid them no mind. None of them bothered him. Truthfully, he cared little for any of them. He merely existed with them rather than connect on any meaningful level. Over-burdened nieces and nephews had forced the retirement village upon him. When he lost his house to an accidental fire, Wesley understood their reluctance to take him in and accepted his sentence to the last home he would ever know.

No loved ones were left to look after him. No siblings were still around, and no spouses or children from a life well-lived. He knew better than to think that way. His life had been one of necessity and little more. His choices had left him empty—an old man without purpose or direction.

The episode cut to a breaking news update. Wesley leaned forward as the news anchor took over the feed.

"A sudden storm surprised a neighborhood in downtown Bethesda tonight. But one unlike any storm we've seen before."

Wesley stopped listening. The hype behind the promo was nothing more than a distraction from the image displayed on the monitor. A storm had passed through earlier in the evening. The heavy rains had now dwindled, but he'd noticed nothing involving lightning.

Amateur video caught the lightning on their phone. They were not streaks of white, brightening up the darkness of the city, but bursts of purple crashing to the street. They left scorch marks on the pavement in the shape of a circle.

"No," Wesley muttered. His hand shook, and the remote slipped from his grasp. The power button connected with the ground, and the television turned off. Grumbling rose from those around him. Wesley, however, remained locked on the blank screen. He still saw the streaks of purple lightning. "No, it can't be."

He pushed off the couch, unaware of his surroundings. His shaking hand slammed into the elbow of another resident. Her pills scattered from her grasp, and joined the remote on the ground. She nearly tumbled herself, but was caught by another patron of the home.

"Fuller!" the woman snapped in anger. "Look what you did!"

Wesley made his way to his feet, then shifted away from the debris strewn carpet. "An accident, Etta. I—"

"It's Edna, you idiot!"

Terrence, the attendant in the room, started over. The doctors in the hall stopped their discussion to check out the scene as well—always watching and judging from a distance. It was like a great social experiment for them as they waited to see who would die next and how.

"What's going on here?" Terrance asked.

The elderly gentleman at Edna's side used the couch to help him get down on his knees to collect the fallen objects. Neither Wesley nor Edna made any such move.

"Wes?" Terrance turned to the still shaking resident with concern.

"It can't be him," Wesley whispered under his breath. He ran his shaking hands along his cheeks. "Not now. Not after so long."

The crouched man retrieved Edna's pills and held them out for her. She shook her head in refusal, which caused her savior to sigh at his efforts. He passed them to Terrance, then snatched the remote off the floor. The television returned to life as the man sat on the couch.

"He went mental," the man said. "As usual."

"Now Ed—"

Ed didn't sound right to Wesley. He had been thinking Frank or George.

"My pills," Edna cried. "All my pills!"

"I'll take care of the pills, Edna," Terrance said in a calm voice. He left Wesley's side and helped her join Ed on the couch. "You know your heart can't take another episode. Sit down and relax."

She nodded. Wesley shifted for a window at the front of the room, where he caught her reflection pointing at him. "He's a menace. He's always been a menace."

Wesley pushed her words away and settled against the window. The glass was cool to the touch from the rain, which still came down in spits and starts. The wind was more of an issue; tree branches swayed violently toward the home.

Terrance's hand settled on Wesley's shoulder. The big man had always shown Wesley a degree of respect no resident ever had. Good people still lived in the world, and Terrance topped the list in Wesley's view.

"Wes?" Terrance called. He tried to pull him from the window, but Wesley resisted. "Come on, let's get you—"

"He's back," Wesley said. "The monster is back."

The concern in Terrance's eyes grew. Voices picked up behind them, calls from more attendants fresh to the room. Terrance waved them over, his focus never leaving Wesley.

"Okay, Wes," Terrance said. His hands clasped on Wesley's arms. Slowly, he guided his attention away from the window. "Let's get you to your room. You need some sleep and—"

Wesley pushed off the strongman. The sudden shift caused Terrance to stumble back a step, colliding with the edge of the card table surrounded by three residents.

"Don't you see?" Wesley said. "He's coming for me! He's always been coming for me, and now he's found me!"

All eyes fell on him. Even Ed and Edna's, though there was no concern to be found in their cold stares, only excitement as a trio of staffers surrounded Wesley. He tried to break away from them for the exit. He didn't need to sleep—not now, not with what was out there looking for him. The nightmare of his youth that had plagued him for so many long decades was back.

Couldn't they see what was happening?

Terrance's hands clamped down on Wesley's shoulders. Mammoth fingers locked Wesley in place and ended his brief escape attempt. The other two guided Wesley to a waiting cot to take him to his room for the night. No one spoke up in his defense, the only voices heard being those from the couch.

"He didn't even apologize for my pills," Edna said with her nose in the air.

Ed grumbled against the cushion of the couch. "Lousy ingrate. Always hogs the remote, too."

The attendants wheeled him out of the common room. Terrance kept him locked against the sheets. Wesley tried to squirm free; his panic caused him to scream into the darkness of the home.

"You don't understand," he said with wide eyes. "He's come to kill me! To kill us all! How can you not get that? Don't you see?"

They ignored him. Each attendant focused on the procedures in place. Wesley had observed each as they were done on others in the home. He had always tried to be quiet, to keep to himself. Now it had cost him a chance to explain what was happening—what was waiting for them all in the dark.

The attendants lifted Wesley from the cot to his own bed. Terrance tried to settle his nerves. Wesley grabbed the man's arm and pleaded for him to understand.

"He's back," Wesley said. "We're all doomed."

Terrance turned to one of the others and nodded. "Right. Better grab that sedative."

Wesley surrendered to their care and to the needle that slipped into his arm. His vision blurred, but he could still see the flashes of lightning. He knew what was coming, and why, as he fell into a deep sleep.

I'm doomed.

CHAPTER THREE

"Are we there yet?"

Morgan Dunleavy wondered how many more times she would hear the incessant whine of Ben Riley's voice before they reached their destination. He only did it to engage—a conversation starter, he called it. To her, it was nothing more than filling an awkward silence.

He had been that way since his return. For the joy and jubilation that consumed those first moments after learning he had survived his brush with death, concern and worry followed quickly. Every glance in his direction confirmed he was indeed back, that the damage wrought by Sullivan's coup and Hendricks' brutal torture was gone. All evidence of the pain Ben endured had been brushed aside and tucked away by a miracle drug.

A drug injected by the Witness, of all people.

That fact scared the living hell out of her. Just knowing the man was involved, after everything he had done in Bellbrook and since, troubled Morgan to no end. Ben tossed her concerns aside. There was nothing left to say on the subject in his eyes. He was back. It was time to move on. She couldn't. Not by a long shot.

"Morgan, I'm serious," Ben said over the whipping wind and the choppy waves beneath the scow of the boat. "Are we there yet? All this bouncing around isn't great for my delicate constitution."

The jokes he made played into her concern. There was always a dig about his health, something that mattered to her. To Ben, however, it was a way to lighten the mood. More accurately, his joking lightened his own mood—never hers.

"Up ahead," she finally said, not bothering to look at him.

"This is the place?" Ben shifted to her side. He removed his sunglasses and squinted through the brightness of the day at the oil rig in the distance.

"According to Adler," Morgan said. Their rental boat skidded across the surface of the Gulf of Mexico. As the massive legs of the rig loomed closer and closer, Morgan slowed the boat to let it settle along the side of the dock installed for incoming travelers. "She hasn't been able to get far with the intel we managed to get from Sullivan and Stallworth, but this place raised a ton of red flags."

Three weeks, and they barely had a blip of a lead on the Trust. Sullivan and Stallworth, for all their duplicity, had kept a tight leash on any viable intelligence for the DSA to glean. Most of the conversations recorded amounted to nothing more than gloating over their successes. They never named those involved with the Trust, or their strongholds.

Three weeks of waiting. The delay wasn't Adler's fault. She was built for logistics, not decryption. When she stumbled across the intel for this place, Morgan jumped at the chance to head into the field.

She was glad for something to do, and she could tell Ben felt the same. He leaped from the boat to the waiting dock. Morgan tossed him a rope. He secured it around the post at the end of the dock, and Morgan killed the engine of their rental.

Ben helped Morgan from the boat, then pulled his sidearm out. She followed suit, and the pair started for the stairs leading to the top of the rig.

"How the hell could a place like this be buried right in the DSA's overhead and Metcalf didn't notice?" Ben said. Morgan wondered the same thing. They all missed too much of late. "I mean, what did the list look like exactly? Paperclips, printer paper, and—oh, yeah—an oil rig? I feel like we're going to find someone inside wearing an eye patch and stroking a cat."

Morgan pushed past him as they reached the deck. Her Glock settled against her palm. She rolled her eyes at him. "He had a scar, not an eye patch."

The landing pad occupied much of the open space on the rig's surface. The platform led to a lower level, where twin double doors sat ajar. Morgan headed for the shadows. She waved for Ben to follow.

"All I'm saying is watch out for booby traps and sharks with laser beams on their heads," Ben continued, his voice quieter as they entered the station's interior.

"Anything to hear yourself say booby."

Ben laughed. The sound echoed through the darkened corridors.

Morgan held up a finger for quiet. "Grow up, Riley."

He passed her his flashlight, and she took it to light the way. "That ship has sailed."

"Along with any chance of an actual conversation, right?"

Ben's smile faded. "Not this again. I'm fine, Morgan."

"Sure." It was the same answer he had given since his return. She had pressed him for an examination, for further study of what the Witness had done to him, yet he remained obstinately against it.

Refusing to rise to the bait, Morgan bit back the mounting questions swirling through her thoughts. She focused on the task instead. They headed deeper into the confines of the rig. The initial entrance appeared to be standard fare for such a setup. Bare walls and pipes ran along the sides. After the first turn, that changed to white walls and signs documenting directions throughout the complex.

The place appeared to be more medical research facility than oil rig. Laboratories of study occupied every corridor. Multiple avenues of study were mentioned on the signage throughout the place. None staggered them more than the name adorning the top of the main double doors to the complex: THE ARK.

"It can't be," Ben muttered. Both knew of the place from Metcalf's debriefing after their time in Chicago during the Promethean affair.

"Come on," Morgan said. "There must be something left behind."

She was wrong. Despite the massive complex, filled with multiple labs on different levels throughout the place, nothing remained from the previous tenants. Every room, be it storage or lab, had been picked clean. Computers were taken or destroyed. The pair of DSA agents found not one scrap of evidence to share with their colleagues back home.

That wasn't the worst of it, though. No, that came from what the previous occupants of the rig did leave behind, and what the pair of DSA agents found as they entered the Cryogenics lab. The occupied tubes were gone, but the names attached to each remained mounted to placards at the base of each station.

One drew Morgan's attention immediately. "Jake..."

Jacob Grissom had brought her into the DSA. He had saved her life and shown her a way to continue to make a difference. Everything she'd known about the man had turned out to be a lie. He had betrayed the DSA, and her in the process. Still, the sight of his name—his body no doubt kept on ice here for months—saddened her.

She turned to Ben, who was standing before the neighboring station. "Hendricks made a comment about it, but I didn't believe him."

"What do you mean?"

He stepped away. The flashlight illuminated the name emblazoned on the placard. "Henry Reed was here. I thought we saved him, but all we did was put him in danger."

She reached for him, a hand on his shoulder. "We'll find him."

Ben pulled away. He widened his arms to showcase the room. There were dozens of empty stations, and names none of them recognized. "And the rest?" Ben asked. "How the hell did we miss this?"

"By not asking the right questions."

Ben took her meaning. "I said, I'm fine."

"I don't believe you," she pressed. "How have you been sleeping? Any dizzy spells? Dietary changes? These are things we should be monitoring, Ben. The Witness—"

"Saved my life," Ben said. "Don't ask me why. Don't ask me how. He did it. And I really am fine, Morgan. Trust me."

"I... I do, Ben, but—"

"Good," he said, not caring to continue the conversation. "Then can we finish up here? This place gives me the creeps."

"Me too," Morgan agreed with a nod. She led them back through the labyrinth of halls until they could see daylight. Ben pushed ahead through the last doors, where the wind washed over him like a wave of fresh air. Morgan slowed to watch. Something was different about him. It was more than being saved by the Witness.

When she joined him in the center of the landing pad, his hands were at his hips and he was letting the sunlight wash over him, like he needed to be cleansed from the operation that had been concealed in the abandoned rig.

"We need to make this right," he said.

"We will," Morgan replied. He ran his hands over his face. "Hey. Ben, we will. You know that."

Ben's dusty brown eyes met hers. A slight nod escaped him. "Let's go. There's nothing here anymore."

She stopped him at the stairs. "I'm not trying to push, Ben, but I'm here if you need to talk."

"Morgan—"

"This is more than just the Witness thing," she said. He might not have wanted to talk about it, but he needed to hear her, truly hear her without the usual sarcastic wit that divided them. "I'm here when you're ready. You know that, right?"

"I..." Ben hesitated, then let out a long breath. Before he could continue, Morgan's phone chirped in her pocket. Ben offered a wry smirk. "Saved by the call."

Morgan grimaced. "I'm not done, Ben." She pulled her phone loose, swiped to accept the call, and placed it on speaker. "What's up, Adler?"

"Catch you at a bad time?" Alison Adler asked. "I can—"

"We're fine," Morgan started. "There's—"

Ben jumped in, leaning closer to the speaker. "The Ark, if I have to call it that, has been cleared out. These Trust bastards are ten steps ahead of us."

"For now," Morgan added.

"Sorry the lead didn't work out," Adler said.

"Not your fault, Adler," Morgan said. "What's going on?"

"A situation has come up at the Bunker."

Ben rolled his eyes. "Another great name. Should we name the boat on the way back to port?"

Morgan turned off the speaker and shifted the phone to her ear. She pointed down the stairs, then started for the boat. Ben stomped petulantly along the metal grating. It was going to be a fun trip back, for sure.

"What's going on, Adler? Is everything okay?"

"New mission," Adler answered. "And you're not going to believe where it came from."

CHAPTER FOUR

His dreams haunted him. Turbulent nightmares persisted whenever he closed his eyes. They stuck with him throughout the night, causing his body to shift and sweat along the fitted sheets.

What they said, what images kept Zac Modine from achieving a restful sleep, remained a mystery. They were feverish, and flashed behind his eyes like a stream of photos, but none ever stuck around. One second his head had hit the pillow and the next the daylight slipped between the blinds to welcome him to the morning.

Zac stretched, his body a never-ending stream of aches on the hard mattress. He turned to his right to offer a morning kiss to his wife, only to be greeted by the wall. Papered daffodils ran in long streaks with lavender lace trim. The sight caused Zac to blink hard to wipe away his confusion. His hands went to his eyes to peel away the night and the shock of waking up in a strange place.

When he shifted away from the wall, there was a figure at the door. Lanky, wearing a denim vest and ripped jeans, the young man tapped casually at his phone. He never gazed up at the half-naked man in the bed, never bothered to knock to gain entry to the room. He simply stood there, the phone more interesting to the seventeen-year-old.

"You're late for work again," Micah Vroman said.

"Huh?" Zac's voice caught in his throat. He turned for the clock to confirm the news. The sudden shift ripped the comforter loose from the bed and Zac fell in a clump on the floor.

Micah took one step into the room. His phone clicked off a

picture, then his fingers were back to dancing along the keyboard. He shook his head as he departed.

"Dumbass."

Zac waited for the footsteps to start down the stairs before he grabbed for the clock. He needed a damn lock on the door. The clock fell from the nightstand and slammed into his chest. The alarm was turned off, even though he knew he had set it the night before.

"Crap," Zac muttered. "Did I turn it off in my sleep? Again?"

His head felt like a pool of muck. The flashing of images remained in his mind's eye, yet he failed to make a lick of sense from any of it. All he wanted was a decent night of rest. Once upon a time, he had worked for days without sleep. His work had kept him engaged, enthralled, and enthused.

All it did now was remind him of how he used to matter. His time at the DSA was sorely missed. From the mundane chatter in the corridors to the clicking of keyboards in the hub, Zac missed his old life.

He was a nobody now, lost in the world. It was his choice, and one he understood at the time, but every morning he woke up in the strange rented room in Connecticut, and failed to remember where he was or how he'd ended up there.

The decision had been necessary. Morgan had cut him off. There was no lifeline back to his old position at the DSA, no friends to rescue him. It was the cost of his inaction. Lincoln's death cemented that. Zac was on his own.

He had found the rental in the paper, one left in the corner booth of a diner at the Massachusetts border. A room was available in exchange for help around the house and a small monthly fee. The woman of the house was a widow — happy with the life her deceased husband's insurance policy allowed for her, but needy as well. Her son, Micah, had his own needs, but they tended to be more in the realm of social media and less in the reality of their crumbling familial bond.

Zac paid for the month, the next already on the horizon. He had meant it to be a brief stay, a chance to reflect on his betrayals — both to the DSA and to his wife — but more and more he found himself too exhausted from the day to focus.

Dressing quickly, a pair of jeans and the same shirt as the day before, Zac headed for the bathroom. A splash of water rinsed the exhaustion from his eyes and matted down the unkempt flecks of hair that marked his beard. Shaving fell away, as did so many other items in his daily routine. He was late for work, after all.

The dishwasher position wasn't ideal. It was quiet, though. He spent hours at the diner down the block from the Vroman home to reconcile his broken life. All in the hope of answering the questions he had raised by his own misdeeds. No answers ever came, only the self-recriminations of a man so lost in the dark he wasn't sure he would ever find the light of day again.

Nancy Vroman stood at the counter. She perked up at his arrival, a constant smile on her plump face. "There he is," she said. "My big helper."

"Now, Ms. Vroman, I—"

"Nancy," the woman interrupted with the shake of her head. She pointed to the pulled-out chair at the kitchen table. "Food's been waiting for you."

"You didn't have to." Zac's stomach churned at the sight of the runny eggs and buttered toast. His appetite had been off for days.

"Nonsense," Nancy replied. "I had to thank you for working on the toaster yesterday. It's like a brand-new machine."

Zac nodded, then took a seat. He lifted the fork beside the plate, but made no move for the food. "You don't have to thank me."

"Rent money would help more," Micah said. His gaze remained locked on the phone in his grip. He bumped into Zac's chair. The impact caused the fork to slip from Zac's fingers and clatter against the table. Micah grinned, continuing for the counter and his waiting lunch.

"Micah!" Nancy shouted, aghast at his behavior. She pointed for the door. "School. Now."

Micah leaned over toward his mother, his eyes never leaving the screen. Nancy kissed his forehead with an exhaustive sigh on her lips.

"Later, Ma," Micah said. He headed for the door, the mutter on his lips clear for their house guest. "Dumbass."

The door slammed shut. Nancy grabbed a dishrag and squeezed it at the shadow of her departing son. "That boy," she grumbled. Her hands came to rest on the edge of the counter.

"You need a lift to the diner, Zac?"

"I'm fine, thank you," Zac answered. He started to stand. "I should get moving too."

Nancy waved him back down. "A few minutes to eat won't hurt you. You're getting too skinny."

She wasn't wrong. He was practically swimming in the shirt he'd purchased at Goodwill just the previous week. Yet the food remained on the plate, the fork by his side.

Nancy grabbed her purse. The strap settled over her shoulder. She tucked her coat under her arm. "I have some errands to run, so lock up when you go. Oh, and the coffee machine could use some loving when you have a chance. It's making some weird knocking sound."

"I—"

"I know," Nancy continued over him. "It's always something. I'm a mess with gadgets. Thank God you're here to help."

Zac offered a weak smile. "Not a problem."

"Perfect," she said. "See you tonight."

The door closed. Zac waited for the engine of her car to start before standing. He watched the SUV back out of the driveway and turn for the street. The quiet settled over the room.

His breakfast waited for him: eggs and toast. He had made the same for Claire the day he'd told her the truth about his affair with Morgan. Zac lifted a piece of toast and nibbled at the corner. His stomach churned louder at the taste.

Lifting the plate, Zac took it to the waste can tucked under the sink and dumped the meal. Nancy tried. He appreciated the attempt, appreciated the opportunity she afforded him by letting him stay in her home and eat her food, but it didn't take away from the strangeness of the place.

It wasn't home.

Zac cleaned off the plate in the trash, rinsed it in the sink, and then placed it in the dishwasher. He wondered what Claire and Alex were up to this morning. If Alex had actually eaten his breakfast or played with it, as was usually the case.

Images of his boy caused him to smile. The moment failed to last as reality crashed down upon him. Zac's shoulders slumped forward, and he sighed.

This wasn't the life he wanted. It was the cost of the one he tried to make through his own selfish deeds. He needed to prove he could be better, that he could be the man he once was — for his wife and son.

Staring out into the sun's gleaming rays, the quiet of the house filled him.

"*Zac…*"

He spun around at the sound of the voice. "Hello? Nancy? Micah?"

The room was empty. The voice was gone.

"Huh." Zac ran his hand through his hair. As his wrist passed his eyes, he noticed the time on his watch. Zac snapped to attention and nearly slipped as he raced for the door. "Crap. I'm really late."

CHAPTER FIVE

Morgan took the lead into the Bunker. She had been leading since the night Ben was shot. Almost without realizing, Morgan had held him in reserve, silently watching over him without being asked or without even questioning her own actions. He grew tired of it.

Honestly, Ben tired of pretty much everything. The lack of leads over the last three weeks ate at him. The Trust remained an elusive beast; the secret organization hid in the shadows, waiting to pounce on them when they least expected it.

Ben wanted to strike back, to inflict the same level of pain that had been put on him. If Hendricks was to be believed, the Trust had been the reason Ben lost his life in Buffalo. That loss also had the unintended consequence of Emily Wright's disappearance—his former partner on the force. He had been trying to correct that situation since receiving Metcalf's offer to join the DSA. It all seemed too far away. He wondered if he would ever reach that goal.

Adler paid no attention to their arrival. She sat with her back to them, while she tapped away against a twin keyboard set up before two large screen monitors. She tied her thick brown hair into a ponytail along the back of her neck. They could hear her fingers dancing across the keys from the far side of the underground complex.

Morgan's eyes thinned as they approached. "What are you doing, Adler?"

Adler jumped from her seat. "I didn't hear you come in." She quickly turned off the far monitor, then spun to greet them. "Nothing. Side project."

Before Morgan could probe deeper, Ben jumped ahead in line. "So that means we have time for a shower and a nap?"

Morgan's frustration at Adler faded, her focus now on Ben. "Feeling tired?"

"And stinky," Ben remarked. "Want to make a federal case over it?"

"Aching bones?" Morgan pressed. "Any trouble breathing?"

Ben swatted at her, then shot down the small stairwell to the monitor womb. "Don't start, Morgan."

"I didn't."

Adler smiled politely through the exchange. Her hands folded in her lap. "Do you two need a minute?"

She was an unlikely member of the team. Innocent to a fault, yet Ben had seen her craftier side when she'd helped him escape a surveillance operation at a local mall months earlier. Adler was certainly a capable agent. Her demeanor, though, made her an oddity. She was still hopeful. Ben wished he felt that way, even a little.

"What have you got, Adler?" Morgan let the concern drop. They needed to finish the conversation, but both were afraid to start. Instead, she moved for the monitor. Adler blocked her from the recently turned off screen to draw their attention to the one still on. "Is this the new op you mentioned?"

"No," Adler replied. "No, this is something else."

Both waited for more. They had flown in for this meeting. The least Adler could provide was some damn clarity. Their furrowed brows were clear to the demure analyst, who cleared her throat.

"Okay," she started, with a clap of her hands. "You were there when the Cove imploded."

Morgan rolled her eyes. "I vaguely recall barely escaping with my life."

"You always have the best times without me," Ben interjected with a wry smirk. Morgan's arms crossed her chest, and her heel softly beat against the floor.

"Anyway," Adler continued. "When the cliff collapsed in on itself, there was this massive electromagnetic discharge. Not unusual in these situations."

"Nope," Ben chided. "Totally normal."

"Riley," Morgan intoned.

Ben took a step back and bowed his head. "Shutting up now. Sorry, Adler."

Adler chuckled. She was still new to their routine. "I monitored the discharge and found this embedded in the readings."

Adler activated the speakers with a single keystroke. Static followed a low whoosh of white noise. The sound wasn't the random static found on a television that had lost reception. This was more targeted, as if there was more to it deep within the noise.

Ben leaned closer. "What is it?"

"A radio wave?" Morgan said.

Adler pointed to Morgan and nodded. "Outside the standard bands. I've been trying to track down the source of the signal without success."

"It's still present?" Morgan put her ear to the speaker to pick up any of the ambiance of the sound. She was clearly getting sucked into the mystery, and her enthusiasm caused him to smile.

Despite the setbacks they had endured, wonder remained part of the job. Sometimes it seemed hard to imagine, but when it came out of something as simple as a mysterious radio signal of unknown origin, Ben remembered why he stayed with the DSA.

"Is the signal localized? Something to do with Blue Hill?"

Adler shook her head. "No. It's global." Morgan's eyes widened. "Yeah. That was my reaction as well. It also explains why I'm having trouble isolating the source. That's my fun for the day. Yours is much cooler."

"Than a ghost signal hidden from detection?" Ben said. "Don't spoil us, Adler."

"Can't help it." Adler stood and pushed through the pair to the waiting monitor on the other side of the conference table. "Take a look at this."

A CCTV feed depicted the front door of a US Postal Service branch. A brick wall led to the double glass doors. Adler zoomed in on the bricks to show one in the center decorated by a small glyph. It was the image of an eagle, turned upside down.

"What are we looking at here?" Morgan asked.

"A dead drop," Adler explained. "Built in the wall of a post office branch. When the eagle emblem on the brick is reversed like this, it's a sign that there's a deposit. Works great for intel gathering or to pass along urgent messages."

"Sounds old school," Ben said. Morgan threw him a glare. "People still say that. Shut up."

Adler waited for a rebuttal from Morgan. Silence was the answer, however, so she continued. "It is by most standards. When you can transmit data over your phone in a matter of seconds, this might look archaic, but it's safer. And freaking cool if you're a Bond fan."

Ben opened his mouth to share his earlier comment at the Ark. He knew Adler would appreciate his humor. Morgan, however, cut him off first.

"Not a word, Riley," she grumbled. Adler cocked an eyebrow for clarification, and Morgan shook her head. "It's nothing. Continue."

"Who does the drop belong to?"

Adler's grin grew at the question. "That's the thing. It hasn't been used, according to our records, since 1982. Before then? It was a DSA dead drop."

"But in those days—"

"There was no warehouse," Adler said over Morgan's question, reading the woman's thought. "No analysts or bureaucracy of any kind. It was just agents passing along tips and cases to investigate. Dozens around the country questioning the status quo and feeding their insights to others using these well-placed locations."

"Where are we talking about, Adler?" Morgan said, unable to take her eyes off the screen. "Is it—"

"Local, yes," Adler answered. Her enthusiasm got the better of her, and when she saw the frustration building in Morgan at being interrupted, she settled herself against the side of the desk.

Ben shifted between them. "Who would have access to this drop? Agents are few and far between these days."

"Too true," Adler replied. "These days."

She moved for the keyboard. Her fingers executed commands barely able to be seen by the onlookers.

"I hacked the feed, and found this." The timestamp was from the previous day. The screen showed an elderly man approach the wall. He waited patiently as more patrons slipped inside. When he was alone, he lifted the brick out of the wall. He tucked an envelope inside, then re-inserted the brick, this time upside down. The man shuffled out of view. "His name is Wesley Fuller. In 1972, he and his partner were some of the first field agents of what would become the DSA."

"Any idea what he left?"

"Yeah," Adler said. She pointed to the envelope on the table. "Not sure who wired the drop to our systems, but it pinged the second he removed the brick. I took a trip there this morning to see what it was."

Ben opened the envelope and took out the letter inside. *"I need help. He's come back and I need your help."*

"Who's back?" Morgan asked.

"No idea," Adler said. "There's no real data from that time beyond his name and this image from the Archives."

She brought up the photo of a young man in his late twenties. He stood in a tan trench coat, with messy chestnut hair and a thin face. Sharp brown eyes stared out at them. They matched the eyes of the old man from the post office footage.

"That's all?"

Adler shook her head. "I did also manage to find his current address. If you're interested in helping, that is?"

Ben stared at the letter. Someone needed their help. More than just a random person, this was a former DSA agent. It wasn't the Trust, though, and that was where their focus needed to be, wasn't it?

"Pass it off to Metcalf and Kanigher," Ben said. "Where the hell are they, anyway?"

"Out," Adler said. "They didn't tell me where they were going."

"Of course not," Ben muttered. "Well, I think…" Ben fell silent at the sight of the excitement in Morgan's deep eyes. "I think Morgan's made up her mind already."

"I'll drive."

Ben sighed. "So, no nap?"

Morgan shook her head. "We leave in ten minutes."

CHAPTER SIX

Ben negotiated for an extra five minutes. He wanted a quick shower and a shave. Morgan couldn't argue with that. With Ben out of the room, it left her free to confront Adler.

"Show me," she said after the room emptied.

Adler's brow furrowed. "The signal? I still haven't been able to isolate the correct frequency, let alone find a point of interaction to trail it to its source. Maybe given a few more weeks, I can—"

"Not the signal." Morgan leaned close and lowered her voice. "The other search you've been trying to hide from everyone. Especially me."

"Morgan..."

The senior agent refused to bend, refused to even look away. "Show it to me. Now."

Adler offered a slight nod, then shifted to the second screen at her station. The display blinked on to show random data points from Blue Hill down to the surrounding areas.

"How did you figure it out?"

"I've helped in the hub enough times to know a recursive algorithm."

Adler turned away from the monitor, hands up in defense. "I know things didn't end the way we wanted them. But Zac didn't deserve what—"

"He earned everything that happened to him," Morgan snapped. "You're actually trying to find him?"

"Of course," Adler said. "He's part of the team."

"Not anymore." Morgan pushed off the desk. The frustration built in her chest. She had left Zac in Maine after the destruction of Sullivan's base of operations. He had sided with the man who had led to the downfall of the DSA. Zac had claimed it was a mistake, but after everything he'd confessed? Morgan hadn't been in a forgiving mood, and the feeling continued every time she thought about him.

"I know you're upset with him," Adler said. "He screwed up. He shouldn't be left out in the cold for a mistake."

"A mistake?" Morgan seethed. "You think this is over some error in judgment? Lincoln is dead!"

"That's not Zac's fault."

"Why? Because his hand wasn't on the trigger?" Morgan felt the heat rising along her body. She slammed her hands on the conference table. "He may as well have for all the good he was. He stood by and let it happen. Zac didn't do a damn thing to save Lincoln. And then, what did he do? Did he speak up, stand against his murderous boss? No, he continued to follow him. He stayed with him, doing everything asked of him. That's not a mistake. That's a whole series of errors that stem from some-thing more than ignorance, Adler. He can't be trusted."

Adler removed her glasses and set them on the desk. She stood, rubbing her eyes. "You weren't there, Morgan. None of us were."

"It wouldn't have changed things. He made his choices."

"Including what happened between the two of you?"

"What?"

A slight smile crept in the corner of Adler's mouth. "You two weren't exactly the sneakiest people on the planet."

"That's not what this is about."

"I think it has more to do with it than you want to admit," Adler said. "Zac wasn't a saint. I can attest to that. There were times I wanted to smack him upside his head so he would focus on the work, like he did before I joined his department."

"Before Metcalf planted you in his department, you mean."

Adler nodded. It had been an obvious ploy from the former director. Zac had needed oversight. A rift had grown for weeks following the Promethean affair. Adler had been an innocuous plant, able to do the job, while also filtering intel up the chain without Zac's knowledge.

"It wasn't what I wanted," Adler said. "I hoped he would see me as more than that. Instead, my presence just drove a deeper wedge in the trust he once held for Susan and for the department. What happened to him is as much my fault. What he did—"

"No," Morgan said. "Not even close. You did your job, and you did it well. Zac? Zac was always going to make his choice. There was nothing either of us could have done."

"That doesn't mean I won't stop trying." Adler returned to the monitor to retrieve her glasses, and slipped them back on.

Morgan shifted behind her. The search continued on the screen. No hits showed; there were no sightings of her former lover. "I know. Just... be careful, Adler."

"You too."

Morgan left the analyst to her work. The weight of her own mistake followed her up the stairs from the monitor womb. Zac had been an error in her own judgment. Their time together, while wonderful, clouded everything. She refused to let that happen again.

"Everything all right?" Ben asked. He ran his fingers through his still wet hair in a rush. Throwing his coat on, he started for the door.

"Everything's fine." Morgan grabbed the keys, then pushed past Ben for the open door and the exit to the Bunker. "Let's get to work."

CHAPTER SEVEN

Susan Metcalf never thought she would make it back to DC. It was too dangerous for her, given her rogue status in the intelligence community. After the fall of the DSA, she was persona non grata—a leper to those she knew as colleagues and friends… not that they were really either.

The people around her were tools to be used to improve the status of her department. Each player in the game was meant for one thing in her eyes: to funnel casework to increase the prestige of the DSA. That mentality helped bring the DSA down, helped crush her dream, and in the process, sent her underground with no chance of returning.

At least, not the way she would have liked.

The game might have changed thanks to Sullivan's betrayal, but Metcalf rolled with the punches. She had planned accordingly, bringing with her the critical components to fight back against the Trust, the organization that had been manipulating her from the very start.

Still, something was missing. With Ben, Morgan, and Kanigher by her side, she had her field team. Adler was perfect for logistics and intelligence gathering. Metcalf remained staunch in her operations acumen, but the technical side faltered in the absence of Zac.

The lack of leads in the wake of Blue Hill attested to that. Adler, while capable with the Bunker's networks, hadn't been able to crack Sullivan's encryptions—those put in place by Zac. In the age of the computer, there was no alternative than to have an expert in the field.

Going through proper channels for recruiting was no longer

an option. She couldn't very well show up at the NSA and offer their top analysts a competitive package with medical, dental, and a kick-ass pension plan. The only thing she could offer was day-to-day danger. It was not exactly the best sales pitch.

With her usual forms of staffing off the table, the door opened to alternative means. Metcalf found her candidate within the first week of searching. She had known the man from his work, and from a few scant conversations years earlier during her tenure as director of the DSA. For the last ten days, Metcalf had done everything she could to track him down.

He stood at the corner of Wabash and Donovan. Jeans torn at the knees and a hoodie covered his spindly frame. He hugged tight to the brick, munching on a hot dog from a street vendor. Thin eyes scanned the block every few seconds. He was nervous, mindful of his surroundings. Cautious to a fault, when he noticed the same sedan circle the block for the second time, he left the corner behind.

Metcalf knew it was time for an introduction. Positioned on the roof across the street, she lowered her binoculars as the young man departed. He wouldn't go far. His travels stuck to known associates and conditioned behaviors, though he would be the last to admit that much. He saw himself as a rebel—unable to be pinned down by conventional means. Metcalf was anything but conventional.

She also wasn't alone.

She had picked up her tail the second she reached DC. He wasn't particularly stealthy, and on the rooftop of the DC Metro hotel, there was little in the way of cover.

Metcalf sighed. She didn't bother to turn around, though she could feel the man's eyes boring holes into her back. "Done stalking me?"

Robert Kanigher joined her at the edge of the roof. "You left the Bunker without a word."

"You should have taken the hint, then." Metcalf shifted away from the ledge, kicking at the gravel set along the rooftop. "I'm busy."

"I didn't sign up to be kept in the dark," Kanigher shot back. "I thought things would be different, Susan."

"They are," she said. "I'm doing everything I can to keep us in the fight."

"By what? Spying on people."

"Recruiting assets," Metcalf said. She held out the binoculars. Kanigher took them in hand and peered down at the street below. "Green hoodie at the end of the block."

Kanigher adjusted his view until he caught sight of the man. He lowered the lenses slowly. "You've got to be kidding me." Kanigher tossed the binoculars at her. She snatched them out of the air. "Nixon Jessup? Are you out of your damn mind?"

"Have you figured out why I didn't tell you where I was going yet?" Metcalf said. She started for the exit. She couldn't let Nixon get too far ahead of them.

"He's a terrorist."

"He claims he's merely a freedom fighter."

"Tell that to the thirty-thousand people who lost their life savings to his hack of the Norwest Bank four years ago," Kanigher railed. "Or how about the train derailment he caused that killed six people?"

"Six criminals," Metcalf shot back. She had done her homework. She knew the truth about Nixon. He was the same as all of them — fractured and broken. "They hijacked the train. He stopped them."

"People died."

Metcalf slammed her hand on the door. "This isn't easy for me, Bobby."

"He's dangerous."

"And we can use him," Metcalf said. "The Trust has us against the wall. On the run. We can't waste time on morality plays. We can't be the good guys every second of every day."

"Then what the hell are we fighting for?" Kanigher asked. His hand lifted her chin so he could meet her gaze. His eyes were tired. She couldn't imagine what her own looked like anymore. "Why are we even doing this?"

"No one else will," Metcalf replied, pushing away from him. She started down the stairs for the ground level. "That's good enough for me."

Kanigher pounded against the steps after her. "Dammit, Susan, hold up."

"He's getting too far ahead. I don't want to lose him. Not now."

"Maybe you should," Kanigher said. "I get what you're saying, but cutting out the team like this? That wasn't what we signed up for, what Jake and I gave up everything to be part of when you asked us."

"Don't." She spun on her heels, a finger raised to his chest. "Don't you dare put that on me. No one asked you to throw away your career. No one asked Jake to…"

She trailed off, her words lost to the stairwell. Jacob Grissom was dead, another victim of their fight. His betrayal still stung.

"Just don't."

"Fine," Kanigher said. He kept his voice soft and slow. "Then let's focus on this Jessup guy. He's a lunatic. I've seen the NSA's files. He's a tin-foil hat conspiracy nut. There are no answers here."

"You're wrong, Bobby." Metcalf pulled the stairwell door open. The noise of the lobby filled the air. It drowned out her frustrated steps along the tile. "You should trust my judgment."

Kanigher's hand fell on her arm, holding her up at the exit. "Why? You don't trust anyone else's!"

Looks rose from passing pedestrians. Kanigher led Metcalf through the breezeway to the sunshine outside. Once away from the milling crowd, he let her go.

"We are facing something we barely understand," Kanigher said, concern in his voice. "People shrouded in shadows with no way of finding them out, and you're putting all your trust and all your faith in a stranger. Instead of us. Instead of me."

Metcalf gaze fell low. "This isn't about us, Bobby."

"Isn't it?"

Metcalf shook her head. She headed for the open street and her reason for coming to DC. "Nixon Jessup is important."

"He's also standing right here."

Both looked up to see the young man leaning against the brick. He sipped at the bottle of soda through a thick straw, a laptop bag strapped tight to his shoulder. Nixon offered a wave and a nod at the pair of surprised agents.

"I hear you've been looking for me."

CHAPTER EIGHT

There were a dozen things Ben considered more important for the use of his day. Laundry would have been a top consideration. The bunker mentality was not conducive to a massive wardrobe, and he had run out of clean socks two days earlier. There was also the fact that the Trust remained at large—the true villains of the story and the only thing that kept Ben going from day to day.

It was about justice for Ben. Their manipulation of the DSA, from Sullivan to Stallworth, kept them from seeing the complete picture. They had also orchestrated his fall from grace in Buffalo. He lost his life thanks to their efforts to suppress the truth from the populace, to hide their clandestine operations. They needed to pay for that. He needed them to pay.

Visiting a senior living facility in downtown Bethesda failed to make the list. It wasn't even on Ben's damn bucket list, let alone his plans for the day. He stewed about it throughout the drive. Morgan tried to pull him into a conversation, but he barely engaged. When the talk shifted to more concerns about his health, Ben stopped answering all together.

"Let's just get this over with."

Before the engine clicked off, Ben was out the door and on his way to the front of the building. He slipped through the crowd outside, trying to enjoy the sunshine and the limited warmth it brought after weeks of chill and snow. Ben nodded casually at the old men and women in wheelchairs, who eyed him oddly as he approached.

Morgan joined him at the entrance. "Everything all right?"

"Fine," Ben replied. He didn't need her concern. "I'm fine,

Morgan."

"Good to know."

A burly attendant sat behind the reception desk. The nametag attached to his white uniform read ERNIE in big, bold letters. He had a youthful smile. "May I help you?"

Morgan removed her badge from her pocket and flipped it open. Ben tried not to wince at seeing the FBI logo. Both were not fans of the subterfuge required for their new positions, but the Trust had given them little choice in the matter. The DSA was dead in the eyes of the public. They needed to play the game differently in order to make an actual difference in the world.

It was one more thing the mysterious group would have to answer for when the time came — if it ever did.

"Agents Dunleavy and Riley," Morgan said. "We're here to see one of your residents. Wesley Fuller."

The smile faded at the mention of the man's name. "What's he done now?"

Ben held back a laugh. "Troublemaker?"

Ernie's hands clenched tight on the desk. "He slipped away from me when we were out yesterday. Took me three hours to find him. I almost lost my job."

Ben and Morgan shared a silent glance. His sudden absence must have come when Wesley delivered his message to the secret dead drop at the post office. The look fell away quickly, and Morgan shook her head at the frustrated attendant.

"It's nothing like that," she said with a disarming smile. "Just routine follow-up."

Ernie hesitated for a moment. Then he pointed deeper into the facility. "Down the hall to the left. He should be in the rec room."

"Sounds fun," Ben commented.

"It's not," Ernie answered.

Morgan prodded Ben down the hall; the attendant's reply caused a smirk on the agent's face. She knew Ben better than to let the man's words hang in the air like that. There was another comment in the making from the ever-sarcastic Ben Riley. She clearly didn't want to hear it, and he was fine to let it pass.

He stepped lively down the corridor. There was no hesitation, no desire to prolong their stay among the elderly. Everyone around him appeared withered and fake, like their smiles were false fronts for the pain they held. Ben certainly understood that. He carried his own since his near-death experience. It caused him to lose sleep for days on end, but it also motivated him to keep moving.

Those days seemed to be long gone for the residents of the Happy Acres Retirement Village. The residents, while content with their every need sought to by the staff, appeared to be killing time until the end rather than doing anything with it.

"Ben?" Morgan shook him from his spiraling thoughts. "You sure you're all right?"

"Peachy," he said, with a smile as fake as the many he saw around him. "Wondering if I should get on the waiting list while I'm here."

"We should be so lucky." Morgan headed into the rec room for a sign of Wesley.

Ben held back a step. She meant what she said. To live a life as long as those in the senior facility was a gift in her eyes. Ben wasn't so sure at the moment. "Lucky." The mutter slipped from his lips. "That's one word for it."

"Come on," Morgan called from inside the room. "I see him."

He sat at one of the three round tables positioned near the windows. Sunlight coated his thinning white hair. Hunched over in his chair, the man picked at the thousand-piece puzzle before him — the project well in hand as they approached.

"Wesley Fuller?"

"Who's asking?" the man responded without looking. The puzzle was more interesting to him. Ben took a seat across from Wesley; his gaze took in every aspect of the former agent. Ben didn't know what he'd expected upon arrival. Age had not been kind to Wesley. His cheeks were gaunt and his skin stretched. Wrinkles dominated every inch of exposed flesh, with liver spots along his neck. Something more glowed in the man's eyes, however: a fire behind wide brown irises.

Morgan displayed her badge once again. "Agents Dunleavy and Riley."

Wesley sat back in the chair. He dropped the puzzle piece, his eyes locked on the badge. His lips curled. "I bet."

A woman at an adjacent table lit up at the sight of Morgan's badge. She nearly toppled from her seat; only her companion kept her from falling to the floor. "Are you here to arrest him? Hot damn, it's about time."

"They're probably here for you, Etta dear," Wesley snapped. "Finally gotcha for hooking on the weekends."

"It's Edna, you senile old fart," the woman said. She turned to Morgan while pointing at Wesley. "He's a horrible old man, and should die in a jail cell."

"Better than this hellhole," Wesley grumbled. Ben couldn't help but agree. An attendant started over, drawn by the arguing between the residents. Wesley waved him away. "Leave me be, Terrance. The old bat started it."

"You know you need to stay away from Edna." Terrance's hands were braced on his hips; his frame towered over the table.

"Yeah, I forgot," Wesley said. "She's a delicate flower, and I'm a psychopath."

Morgan stepped between them. "We'd like to have a few minutes with Mr. Fuller, if you don't mind."

Terrance sidestepped Morgan, moving to the other side of Wesley's chair. He pulled the man away from the table slightly to give him room. "I'd be fine with it, but this curmudgeon has a doctor's appointment, and I drew the short straw to take him. You're welcome to come back this evening."

Ben started to stand. "That will be—"

"We can take him," Morgan interrupted.

"What?" Ben asked, confused. "To his doctor's appointment? Morgan..."

Morgan smiled at the attendant. "It's not a problem."

"It's against procedure, I'm afraid," Terrance said. "Not to mention what a handful he can be."

"We can handle him," Morgan said. "You're welcome to join us if you're concerned for Mr. Fuller's well-being with a pair of federal agents."

"It's not... I didn't mean anything..." Terrance sputtered. "There's no good answer out of this, is there?"

"Just the one I'm looking for, I'm afraid," Morgan replied.

"I really shouldn't... He's—"

"Sitting right here, you bulbous ass," Wesley remarked. "You want to fight them on this?"

Terrance sighed. "Not in the least. I'll jot down the details for you."

"Thanks," Morgan said.

Ben rolled his eyes. Their wasted day just got longer. "Yeah. Sounds like a blast."

CHAPTER NINE

Metcalf led Nixon deeper down the alley to continue their discussion. Kanigher kept his distance. He stuck close to the mouth of the alley, ever the protector, even when Metcalf didn't ask him to be. Bobby had always been that way for her, ever since their first meeting. She had a love-hate relationship with his chivalrous mentality. Today her mood fell to the side of hate, and it took all her willpower not to spell it out for him.

Nixon, though, was the priority. He took ten steps into the alley, then leaned along the side of the hotel. His beat up sneakers scraped along the brick. The straw of his drink tightened between his lips as he took in a long and loud sip.

"I take it you know what this is about," Metcalf started. Ignorance was not the card to play with a man like Nixon. His intelligence was off the charts, his behavior that of someone who knew too much with too little restraint. Knowledge didn't always make him right, however — just arrogant. Metcalf counted on that now.

"Saw my system getting pinged," Nixon said. His dark complexion reflected his Native American heritage. Black, beady eyes looked Metcalf over with curiosity. "It wasn't very subtle."

"Maybe I wasn't trying to be."

Nixon smirked at the revelation. "When I traced it, I realized who it was. I heard you were dead."

"Don't believe everything you read," Metcalf replied.

"I never do," Nixon shot back. "Still… the infamous Susan Metcalf? Now what could she want with little ol' me?"

"Nothing, if I had my way," Kanigher commented from his position at the mouth of the alley. His arms crossed his chest in aggravation.

Metcalf cleared her throat. Kanigher's focus returned to the street instead of their conversation. She offered Nixon a welcoming smile. "I think you can guess why I'm here."

"I remember the last time we met." Nixon left the comfort of the wall, circling Metcalf before sitting along the edge of a dumpster. "You were starting up that… what was it you called it again? A think tank?"

"I was looking for the best."

"Yet you ended up with Zac Modine, of all people." Nixon shook his head in contempt. "Not exactly the top of the class."

"That's not how I saw him."

"What happened, Susan?" Nixon pressed. "Get cold feet after our chat?"

Metcalf fought to keep her jaw from clenching. She didn't like explaining herself. "You were a loose cannon, Nixon. When you push too far, people get hurt. Norwest showed me that."

Nixon let out a loud laugh. "Norwest? One of the largest banks in the world. It caters to millions, yet somehow I only wiped out the savings of 30,000? You know me better than that."

"Who were they?" Metcalf asked. Kanigher's ears perked up to listen as well.

"People who deserved a little loss in their lives," Nixon explained. "Landlords who stole from their tenants. Cops who skimmed off the top from some well-known busts. Crooks and thieves alike."

"Why didn't you tell the public that?"

"I didn't have to," Nixon said. "Every one of them knew why it happened to them. Why do you think the investigation went nowhere?"

"I thought it had to do with a lack of evidence?" Metcalf said. "Somehow, every time a lead popped up, it vanished just as quickly. Like someone was covering their tracks."

"And doing a fantastic job of it," Nixon finished. He took a slight bow, chuckling under his breath. "Tell me about the DSA, Susan."

"What?"

Kanigher shot her a look. "How did he—"

"Oh, come on now." Nixon jumped down from the dumpster. He tossed the rest of his soda into the trash. "A think tank?

Why would you think for a second I would fall for that line? I've been following stories about the DSA since I was in grade school."

Metcalf grimaced. Keeping secrets was her stock-in-trade. She preferred to know more than the people surrounding her. Nixon's information was dangerous, but crucial to the DSA's future success.

"I want you on my team."

"The DSA," Nixon reiterated. "I heard they were defunct. Dead as the dodo."

"You know better than that," Metcalf said.

"Why me? Why now?"

"We're free agents." Metcalf gauged his interest. Nixon's eyes sparked for a second, but he said nothing. Metcalf continued, "No operational support. We work in the shadows now. We might have lost the old DSA, but that doesn't mean the fight is over."

"Altruism?" Nixon said with a scoff. "That's your pitch? Pass."

"Okay."

"Okay?" Kanigher's brow furrowed. "That's it? You just let him walk?"

"Of course," Metcalf said. "If that's really what he wants."

"No benefit and all risk on my part," Nixon chimed in. "Not what I'd call a promotion for me."

"No surprise there." Kanigher moved for Nixon, hands in front of him. They collided with the young man's chest. Nixon slammed into the side of the dumpster. "You've never had to face up to anything in your life. You attack people from behind a keyboard, wiping them out with the click of a button. Ruining lives as it pleases you without a cause. Without a mission."

"I take out the bad guys. Same as you," Nixon spat at Kanigher. "Just in my own way."

"Let him go, Bobby." Metcalf's hand brushed along the man's back.

"You sure?"

Metcalf nodded.

Nixon adjusted his hoodie, then started for the street. "We should do this again in a few years."

"I'm surprised at you, Nixon," Metcalf called after him. "You never asked who we were fighting. What we're after."

Her words stopped him in his tracks. He turned, his disarming and arrogant smile greeting her again. "All right, I'll play. Who?"

"Susan…"

Metcalf ignored Kanigher. "The Trust."

Nixon's mouth fell open. The arrogance was gone, replaced with a deep surprise that washed over his entire body. "The Trust?"

"That's right."

"They're real," Nixon muttered. "I knew it."

Kanigher turned to Metcalf, confused. "He knows about them?"

"I've been after them for years," Nixon said. "I've tried to force them into the light. Reports through official channels. Anonymous tips to precincts around the country, all in the hopes of showing the world what the hell is really going on."

Metcalf nodded. "And each time they were buried and forgotten."

"Yeah," Nixon said. "Meanwhile, I got more heat brought down on me."

"It won't be like that," Metcalf said. "Not if you work with us on this."

"You're crazy," Nixon shot back. "You tell me the Trust is real. I knew it. I've always known it and no one would listen to me."

"I will," Metcalf said. "We will."

Nixon knocked his hood back and ran his hand through overgrown black locks. "They have enclaves in every country. Meetings at the highest level. Have a cell phone? They built it, programmed it, and distributed it to every corner of the globe. Take a multi-vitamin? Their labs concocted the formula, brick by molecular brick. They control your finances, pop culture, and more than half the governments in the world. No one has a clue who they are or what they want.

"No one wants their life to be meaningless. These people prove that to be the case every day. I tried to tell people about them, about what I've seen out there in the world. No one believed me. They called me paranoid. It got to where I didn't even believe it to be true. How could the Trust exist and no one notice?"

"But you were right," Metcalf said. "You've always been right."

"They won't let you win," Nixon said. "They can't let anyone know the truth."

"They don't get a choice this time," Metcalf replied. "Help us, Nixon. Help us bring them into the light."

The hacker backed away to the mouth of the alley. He shook his head, his hands before him. "I'm sorry. I can't."

"Nixon?"

"Too much risk, remember?" His sad eyes met hers for a second before the arrogant smile returned. He reached the end of the alley and started for the open street.

"There he is!" a shout rang out from down the block. Two officers stood in front of the hotel they had exited for their chat. The doorman spoke with them, then pointed toward the alley. Nixon skidded to a halt. Both officers ran toward him.

"Nixon Jessup! Don't move!"

CHAPTER TEN

Nixon stood stock-still at the mouth of the alley. The officers raced toward him, but he could not think and could not act at their violent reaction to seeing him. Metcalf, on the other hand, was already in motion.

She pushed through Kanigher for the young man. Keeping her head low and away so as not to be identified by local PD, Metcalf grabbed Nixon and yanked him into the alley.

"Time to go."

"I don't get it," the young man muttered. He stumbled for the first step, held upright by Metcalf's iron grip on his sleeve. "I disabled the cameras. I took precautions to avoid being seen. How—"

"Analyze later, kid," Kanigher said. He drew his sidearm.

"Bobby?"

"Run." Kanigher cocked his head to the opposite end of the narrow stretch. "I'm right behind you."

She nodded. It was enough for them and a sign of her true trust in him. He may not have believed her on that front, but she trusted him. She had to, or everything else would fall apart. She just wished it went both ways.

Shots filled the air. Metcalf peered back to see Kanigher unload on the approaching officers. The corner brick shattered from the bullets. Both cops dove out of the way. They shouted for backup over the violence.

Metcalf pushed Nixon forward. "My car is on the next block."

Nixon shook his head. "Response time for DC police is—"

"I don't want to know," Metcalf said. "Just keep moving."

Kanigher was still stuck behind them. Every few steps, he turned back to the officers to keep them pinned. It was a delaying tactic at best, and one that would not end well for her colleague.

"Let's go, Bobby!"

"Coming, dear." Kanigher emptied his clip, then darted after the pair. The officers hesitated a moment before they continued their pursuit through the alley.

Metcalf pushed Nixon forward until they reached the adjacent street. Cutting right, the pair almost barreled into a group of pedestrians out for an afternoon stroll. A middle-aged man stumbled against the storefront window to give Metcalf and Nixon enough room to squeak through.

"Sorry about that," Metcalf said in passing.

More cries arose at the arrival of Kanigher. "Pardon me!"

Kanigher's long stride easily overtook them. Within seconds, all three were at the waiting car.

"Get in," Metcalf called.

The officers rounded the corner. Metcalf couldn't take the chance. She pulled out her gun. Her shots were high and away from the pair, but did the job. Driven back into the alley, Metcalf jumped into the driver's seat of the car. The engine roared to life.

"Head down. Let's go."

Nixon complied, and dove for the back seat. Metcalf shifted into drive. The tires squealed in anger. She peeled away from the curb, circling in the opposite direction of the cops even though the road was a one-way.

She caught sight of the officers in the passenger side mirror. They were calling in the car. It wouldn't matter once they made it out of DC. She had plenty of replacement plates in the trunk.

"What the hell was that?" Kanigher asked after they had filtered into light traffic on the expressway heading north. There was no sign of pursuit. Still, Metcalf refused to let up on the gas pedal to the same degree that Kanigher refused to let up on their guest. He hitched his thumb to the back of the car and the cowering Nixon. "Well? What the hell?"

Nixon sat up, fixing his hair with both hands. "I may have a few outstanding warrants."

Kanigher threw Metcalf a look of fury. "Are you kidding me with this? This is the guy you want to have on our team?"

"I haven't exactly agreed to that," Nixon clarified.

"How many options do you have?" Metcalf caught Nixon's eyes in the rearview mirror. Then she turned to Kanigher. "How many do we have?"

"He's a criminal, Susan," Kanigher said. "One hour with him, and we've had a shootout with the police. This is the direction you want to take things?"

Nixon leaned between the seats until he was level with Kanigher's face. "Hey. No one asked you to rescue me. I didn't need saving. I would have been fine on my own."

"Hear that?" Kanigher said. "Let him out here. He's fine."

"Bobby…"

"Don't, Susan. Don't try to sell me on this."

"Fine," Metcalf said. "I'll let him do that for me."

"What?" Nixon asked in surprise.

Metcalf eyed the nearest exit on the expressway and shot over from the far lane at the last second. Horns blared, followed by shouts of anger at passing motorists. Metcalf reached the end of the off-ramp and slammed on the brakes. She let the car idle along the side of the road.

"Precinct is five minutes away," Metcalf said. "That's how this story ends for you, Nixon, if that's the way you want it."

"Or?"

"You help us with the Trust."

Nixon scoffed. "There is no stopping these people. You have to see that."

"I refuse to believe that," Metcalf replied. "Somewhere deep down you do, too. That's why you've pursued them for so long. That's why you kept digging into them, even though you knew it would never end well."

Kanigher shook his head. "Susan, let him go. We'll find someone else. Someone who has the courage to stand up and make a sacrifice."

"You want a sacrifice?" Nixon spat at the man. "You want to see what happens when I stand up?"

"No." Kanigher nodded toward Metcalf. "But she does."

"Fine," Nixon said. "I'll show you what you're dealing with, and what happens when you cross these people."

CHAPTER ELEVEN

"The doctor will be with you shortly," the receptionist of the Wilmut Clinic said. "Please take a seat and someone will call you back in a few."

Plenty of confused glances shot toward the trio with their arrival at the doctor's office. Wesley made no mention of his escorts, though the question had been on the tip of everyone's tongues. Ben let the awkward looks follow them to their seats in the far corner of the waiting area.

Morgan took the seat closest to the window. Wesley sat next to her, then shuffled for the magazines at the table in front of him. He sifted through the massive pile of out-of-date periodicals, bitching the entire time about the selection. Ben grabbed the latest *Sports Illustrated* from the rack near the receptionist desk and tossed it to him.

"Read it," Wesley said. The magazine fell into the graveyard on the table. The old man sat back in his chair, a pout on his face to match the seven-year-old waiting across the way for his shots.

Ben wanted to scream. What the hell were they doing? Wesley wasn't a lead; he was barely a functional adult anymore. Everything in the man's life was monitored and restricted. It was all to keep the man breathing, not living. Didn't that say something about any information he might offer them?

Morgan obviously didn't want to hear from Ben. She stared out the window rather than listen to his frustration at their situation. They should have been working on Sullivan's files, on the drive Morgan stole from Grissom's dead body, anything that might lead them to the Trust. Instead, they were babysitting a geriatric curmudgeon who hated humanity almost as much as

Ben did currently.

Ben shook his head and crashed into the chair next to Wesley. The back bumped into the wall behind them. He grumbled under his breath as he shifted the plastic seat back into position. Looking around the room, almost a dozen patients waited for their turn. Two were children, but the rest matched the less-than-sunny disposition of the man beside him.

There wasn't much to look forward to in life if this was the result. Poked and prodded, all for the chance to eke out another year, while never really getting the chance to do anything else. Nothing filled the days but doctor's appointments and daytime television. Ben shivered at the thought, almost thankful his parents weren't around to experience this side of their twilight years.

"I appreciate the company," Wesley said, breaking the silence between them. "At least yours, gorgeous, but why don't we put our cards on the table?"

"There isn't room," Ben replied. "Too many magazines that you refuse to read."

"Ben," Morgan intoned.

"What, Morgan?" Irritation crept into Ben's voice. "The man has a perfectly good point. What the hell are we doing here?"

Morgan's eyes thinned. Ben slammed his head back against the wall in frustration. Morgan drew closer to Wesley. "As we said, Mr. Fuller, we're—"

"DSA," Wesley finished for her. Both agents turned to the man. "And leave the badges in your pockets. They look like you found them in a Crackerjack box."

"How did you know?" Morgan asked.

Wesley grinned; wrinkles spread from the corner of his lip all the way across his cheek. "I knew the DSA was still around. That speech from the NSA Director... Stallworth? I wondered who put him up to it, who outed the secret department? Who else, right?"

"You seem pretty involved for being retired," Morgan said. Ben pursed his lips, ready to jump in. Retired only took it so far. The man was clearly a mess, his glory days long since over. Why they weren't just asking him the questions and moving on with their day annoyed him to no end, but he let Morgan continue to lead.

"I follow the news." Wesley's body appeared looser in the presence of Morgan. He was enjoying the conversation, something that couldn't be said back at the retirement home. "I read between the lines and lend a hand with active casework when I have something useful to say. When you've been doing the job for as long as I have, it becomes like breathing."

"Look," Ben interjected. He didn't need a summary of the man's life. "We found your message."

Morgan shot him an angry glare. It softened toward the gentleman between them. "What's going on, Wesley?"

"Percival Jenkins." Wesley slipped a hand into his pocket and removed a news clipping. Ben snatched the piece of paper from the man's hand. "He was killed two nights ago."

Ben scanned the article. "Says here it was an animal attack."

"It wasn't an animal."

"How do you know?" Ben asked sharply.

Wesley's cold eyes bore through him. "I do, young man. I've seen this before. The same thing happened the day I lost my partner. Joshua Falk."

Neither Ben nor Morgan replied.

Wesley sighed at their silence. He lifted his hat and ran his hand through his scattered hair. "I know how it sounds. I also know you've both seen stranger, or you're not real DSA. I'm talking about science gone berserk. Things unheard-of. If I had known back then, I probably would have run in the other direction."

The same thought echoed in Ben's own mind. "A smarter person would have, anyway."

Morgan cleared her throat to silence Ben. "We're listening. What happened?"

Wesley nodded. He fell silent for a moment, building up the story in his mind. He took the time to think through events clouded by age. When he was ready, his eyes lit up.

"Tyler Abbott," he started. "He was stealing equipment for an illegal experiment. Falk and I were the only two able to connect the dots, almost like Abbott was being protected from someone on the inside."

"What kind of experiments?"

"Quantum manipulation," Wesley answered. "Time travel."

"Wait," Ben said. "Are you—"

"Just listen." Wesley stood to face both of them. He kept his voice low to avoid the stares from the other patients. "Abbott opened a door into the future. But the portal wasn't stable. I lost Falk, but in his place, there was this beast—this monster. That's what did this to the Jenkins boy. I'm absolutely sure of it."

"You're saying this thing found a way back?"

Wesley nodded. "Somehow, yes. I knew he would. Somehow, I always knew he would. I've been haunted by this thing for fifty years."

"I don't—"

"It's me he wants, Agent," Wesley said over Ben. "I know how it sounds. But you have to believe me. I—"

"Mr. Fuller?" a nurse called from the inner door to the office. "I'll take you back to see the doctor."

Wesley turned toward the voice, then back to his escorts. Ben and Morgan shifted uncomfortably in their chairs.

"Do you…" Ben tried to find the words. "I mean, are you good back there, or do you need some support or…"

"I think I can still turn my head and cough." Wesley cocked his head toward Morgan with a grin. "Unless your partner would like to join me?"

Morgan burst out in a laugh. "I think we'll wait here."

Wesley shrugged, then started for the nurse. Ben watched him depart, lost in the story of the man's trauma and what the hell it meant for them.

CHAPTER TWELVE

Morgan held her breath. She knew what was coming the moment Wesley left the room. Hell, the second he mentioned quantum manipulation, she knew where Ben would take it.

Ben's hand ran across his chin like he was mining the depths for that perfect comment to make. Finally, he turned to her with a smirk.

"Time travel, huh?" His grin grew. "Heavy."

Morgan lifted her wrist, pretending to glance at her watch. "3.8 seconds. A new record."

"For what?"

Morgan sighed. "A *Back to the Future* reference."

"Am I that predictable?" Ben put a hand to his chest.

"It was either that, or a Keanu Reeves-style 'Whoa.'"

Ben stared at her, mouth agape. "That is eerily accurate."

For a moment, Morgan believed they had turned a corner. The slight arguments of the past three weeks were over, and they could fall back into routine. Ben's impatience at their lack of progress faded behind that telling smile; the one that said how everything was going to be all right. That the good guys always come out on top, so put those worries to rest.

Ben had been flailing since his return. His emotions jumped from pure sarcasm to an anger she had only seen in him once before. His frustrations spilled into every conversation. Wesley's involvement hadn't helped in that regard, though why Ben wouldn't even give the poor guy a chance startled Morgan. Ben championed the lost cause. He believed in people.

"So, what are we thinking?" he said, leaning back in his chair. "Is the old man delusional, or does he think this is his last chance for an adventure?"

Morgan scoffed. "Or he's telling the truth."

Ben shook his head, not wanting to hear it. Morgan shifted to the neighboring seat. "What? That option doesn't even make the list?"

"No," Ben said. "It's just… time travel?"

Morgan understood his reticence. She had never dealt with anything like it before, not during her tenure with the department. Nor had there ever been a case like it—at least, that she knew about.

"You don't honestly think—"

"You ever read the old casefiles?" Morgan interrupted. There was no reason to go through it with him, not when he was like this. "I mean, the old, old files from down in the Archive?"

"Never had the pleasure."

"Strange stuff," she continued. "No support from local branches. No Operations for help back at home. These were men and women working cases no one else would touch. On their own time."

"Without authorization," Ben commented. "Without procedure, or due process."

"Like we're doing now," Morgan shot back. "What we have to do to make a difference. Just like Wesley."

Ben stared at the empty doorway leading to the offices in the back. "He was one of the first? Him?"

"With that Falk guy he mentioned," Morgan confirmed. "I never saw much from his time, though. Not sure why." She tried to recall more from her reading, none of which had been recent. Morgan shook the question away and turned to Ben. "Listen. We might have seen some insane crap, but think about what he's been through. We've had the benefit of the computer age, the internet, and modern advances."

Ben chuckled. "And the 70s were the dark ages?"

"A world of difference is all I'm saying. Look what happened to you, for crying out loud. You—" Morgan paused. She stared at the open door and the access to the examination rooms throughout the medical practice.

"Morgan?" Ben asked. "What?"

She grabbed his hand and stood, pulling him along for the ride. "Come with me."

The nurse at the front desk called after them as they passed through the inner door. Her cries were lost in the background. Morgan merely flashed her badge, then continued into the maze of halls that sprouted behind the desk.

They drew stares from doctors and technicians alike, but none spoke out against the two strangers in their midst. Ben tried to resist at first, reclaiming his hand as his own, but he followed her until she landed on their destination: one of the last open rooms in the practice.

It wasn't the typical examination room. A bed was present, but with much more equipment scattered throughout the space. It must have served patients in need of more thorough procedures. The room appeared well stocked to accomplish pretty much anything that might fall under the purview of a general practitioner.

"What are we doing here?"

Morgan pointed to the bed along the back wall. "Take off your shirt."

Ben cocked his head to the side, a hand behind his ear. "Run that by me again?"

Morgan sighed. She closed the door, then started for the cabinetry on her right. A pile of paperwork sat on the counter — reports and drug studies. A man named Simon Holbrook had written each, and the topics immediately drew Morgan in. She flipped through the top one on blood chemistry, surprised at the insights gleaned from a quick peek. Noticing Ben was still fully clothed, Morgan closed the reports and shuffled them back into position.

"Hurry up," she said.

Ben unbuttoned his shirt and tossed it into the empty chair next to the bed. He hopped on the edge. "Is this about—"

Morgan pulled out a fresh needle from the cabinet. Making her way across the room, she closed the door with the swipe of her hand. "You might not care what's floating in your bloodstream from the Witness' miracle drug, but I do. This is too important to ignore, Ben."

"Morgan…" Ben stopped. His fists clenched, and the fight was there for him to start, but he didn't bother. Instead, he held out his arm for her.

"Thank you," she said. Another trip to the supply cupboards

brought with it several test tubes and a blood drawing kit.

Morgan set to work. Ben said nothing as she filled each tube, though she could feel the anger radiating off him. She simply didn't care. She'd almost lost him and wasn't about to do so again by ignoring a potential threat.

While she collected the samples and placed them in an open holder on the counter, the door opened. A tall figure stood in the frame. He wore a white lab coat, his nametag pinned to the lapel. Swollen eyes from a long day and receding brown hair completed the look of the man named Simon Holbrook—if his ID was to be believed.

"E—Excuse me," he said. His voice was shaking to match his hand. "Can I help you?"

"Sure can." Morgan lifted the samples and passed them to the newcomer in the room. She took a second glance at the nametag to make sure she had it right. "Simon."

"What are—"

"I need a full analysis of these samples, Simon," she said. Overwhelming him was easier than explaining the situation. "If you have a test for it, I want it run on these."

Simon held the samples in front of him, confused and disoriented. "You can't just—"

"I can."

Ben removed his badge from his pocket to show the man. "She can."

Morgan nodded. "See?"

"FBI?"

Morgan pointed to the samples. "How long will this take?"

"I… I don't…" Simon took a step back and a deep breath. He put the samples down on the counter, then turned back to the intruders in his space. "Can I see that badge again?"

Morgan removed hers this time and handed it to the man. He swiped at the sweat accruing by his scalp to mat down the few remaining strands of hair. "Morgan Dunleavy?"

The way he said her name struck her as odd. It was as if there was a familiarity not typically held by people she'd just met. "Do we know each other?"

"Huh?" Simon said. He handed her the ID back, but refused to meet her eyes. His gaze centered on the cracked tiles of the floor instead. "No. It's… a beautiful name is all."

Morgan and Ben shared a glance. Ben pretended to push her toward Simon. Ben thrilled at these awkward conversations, especially when they centered on her instead of him. She flipped him off, then moved for the samples. Lifting them up, Morgan placed the samples back in Simon's open hands.

"How long?"

"A… A week," Simon stammered. "But I'm not supposed to —"

"I appreciate it," Morgan said. She nodded to Ben, who jumped down from the bed. "We'll be back then."

She turned for the door, but another presence blocked the way. A short, dumpy woman filled the frame, with an aged face that dripped with anger at the sight of the trio in the room.

"Holbrook!" she shouted. "What have I said about walking off in the middle of a procedure? And who the hell are these people?"

Sweat pooled along Simon's brow. Morgan elbowed him lightly, hoping to prompt a reaction. He read the blow clearly and took in a sharp breath.

"Them?" he started, blinking rapidly. "They are… They're patients. Needing a consult."

"They never checked in," the woman said. "Dammit, Simon, another mistake and —"

"I know, Anne," Simon said. "It won't… It won't happen again."

Anne fumed. More was on her mind, way more baggage between them, but she held her tongue. She stalked off down the hall. Simon moved for the door to watch her leave. Once she was out of sight, he turned back to them, the samples still locked in his grip.

"I have to go."

"One week, Simon," Morgan called after him.

"No problem," he answered, his gaze to the floor and his steps quick to get as far away from the room as possible.

Morgan looked at Ben. He still stood in the center of the room with his shirt off. A wry smirk spread on his face. "Can I get dressed now? Or was there something else you wanted?"

"Dream on, little man," she said with a laugh. "Dream on."

By the time they reached the lobby, Wesley was waiting. He led them out of the office and back to the car. Morgan and Ben said nothing of their activities, though Wesley offered a few of his own theories.

Morgan didn't need to hear much before she stopped him. "Why don't you start from the beginning, Wesley?"

Wesley slipped into the passenger seat, the joking of a moment earlier lost to the sadness of memory. She could see him working through it, like his eyes were open doors to the past.

"It was the first case I ever handled for the DSA. And it was Joshua's last..."

CHAPTER THIRTEEN
April 5th, 1972

"Another late night, Wes?"

Mark Thompson struck a match against the edge of Wesley's desk. He set the flame to the tip of his cigarette to light it. A deep puff was followed quickly by a release that filled the air.

Wesley swatted the smoke. "Yeah, Mark. Just wanted to finish this report."

"There's always a report with you, Wes," Mark said with a chuckle. He dropped the match in the wastepaper basket beside him. The cigarette dangled precariously from his lower lip. "Learn to live a little."

Wesley said nothing. He offered a brief nod before returning to his work.

Mark sighed heavily. "Your loss. Goodnight, Wes."

"Night," Wesley called to the departing agent. Mark slipped through the glass door of the department and into the elevator without a glance back. The fact he tried at all with Wesley surprised the young man hunched over his typewriter. Few bothered with him any longer. Three years at the DC branch had left Wesley with fewer friends than open cases, which, of course, was his reason for the lack of companionship in the first place.

It hadn't always been that way. For most of his career, Wesley had been the quintessential company man. He worked his cases, mingled with his colleagues, and partook in the nightly pastimes of drinking and dining downtown into the late hours. He had made friends with all around him, and they had seen him as a true part of the team.

That had changed over the last six months. It started with the reassignment of one of his cases by the Section Chief, a man named Theodore Duncan. Wesley dealt with fraud on all federal levels. The Billings Bank on Westmont caught his attention thanks to a friendly tip. Deposits came up short, transfers diverted from their intended recipients, and more fraudulent activities had brought Wesley to their doorstep. After a brief questioning, and a sanctioned search of the premises, Wesley had found his smoking gun: written documents concerning the illicit shortening of accounts led to off-shore holdings by several members of the Board of Trustees.

Wesley had brought his findings to his superior, only to find the man more informed than he'd realized. Duncan had always played it straight with Wesley… until that day. As Section Chief, he put a close to Wesley's investigation and reassigned the entire affair to a different division. Wesley called the new agent handling the affair, only to learn the case had been closed.

"Nothing to it," the agent had said plainly.

Wesley had tried to protest, but caught himself. A quiet word of thanks ended the call. From then on, Wesley kept his own counsel. He had looked into dozens of similar cases, some with a connection to the Billings Bank, and others that had been shut down well into the investigation without a word to the wise.

At the closing of the glass door, Wesley found himself alone. He finished typing his stray thought—a legal reason for a search and seizure—then stripped the paper from the typewriter. He set it in the open casefile at his side, closed the cover, and slipped the entire folder into the top drawer of his desk. It would keep until the next morning. Afterhours was meant for an entirely different sort of work.

Wesley pulled out a small keyring from his pocket. Finding the correct key, he slipped it into the lock on the bottom drawer. It swung open with a loud crash, and he cursed his eagerness. A stack of work sat within. Cases from his own department, as well as a dozen others, lifted from the depths of the drawer, and he set them upon his desk with a thud.

"Trying to wake the dead?"

The question caused Wesley to jump from his chair. His hand snatched at his heart. A shadow stepped out from the corner, a smirk the only thing visible on the man.

"Falk," Wes hissed. He shut the drawer, then slammed his key atop the pile of cases in frustration. "You nearly scared me to death. What are you doing sneaking around here at this hour?"

"Perhaps I simply enjoy sneaking." Joshua Falk's grin widened, and he swept across the room with long strides until stopping short of Wesley's desk. "I'm very good at it, at any rate."

"I can certainly attest to that, thank you very much," Wesley said.

Falk worked in Homicide and was Wesley's senior at the agency by eight years. The two men had never spoken until two months earlier when Falk had caught Wesley checking out files not normally under his purview. Wesley had done all he could to avoid the questions that came from Falk, and for a time his attempts had been successful.

It wasn't until landing on one of Falk's closed cases that the pair connected fully. The top suspect of a double homicide that had crossed state lines had dropped off the face of the earth. The circumstances of which had left nothing but questions from Falk, who had sought more action and was promptly refused. Wes, curious of the agent's thoughts on the case, had asked questions of his own. They shared coffee over lengthy discussions, and a bond formed over their shared frustration at the lack of answers.

Falk kept to himself, much as Wesley had since the Billings Bank incident. Over his tenure, Falk had been involved in several high-profile cases. His success rate had been second-to-none, and commendations should have been pouring in from his superiors. It was in his methodology that Falk always faltered. He was reckless to a fault, jumping at leads in the hopes of an arrest. Falk was reviled for his devil-may-care attitude, loud and outspoken when all advice taught him otherwise.

While complete opposites, they found their lives pulled together through the unsolved cases their superiors had shuttered and forgotten for no legitimate reasons over the years. That had been the start of it, at least.

Since their meeting, the pair met regularly to talk about not only the situations that had been swept under the rug, but the ones that had been outright ignored. They were cases of curiosities and bizarre circumstances that screamed for investigation, yet met with nothing but contempt from the official chain of command at the Federal Bureau of Investigation.

"Did you find something out?" Falk pointed to the pile of cases on Wesley's desk, but both knew he meant one in particular: Abbott Technologies.

"I finally heard back from my contact at the company," Wesley confirmed. The lead he'd been waiting weeks for came from the accounting records of Tyler Abbott. Abbott was a businessman of some renown. His technologies firm held multiple government contracts. There was nothing substantial, but enough that his lifestyle made the news once or twice a year for the various functions he attended.

Irregularities had been reported to the local department by some of Abbott's employees. Payments to distributors kept certain elements off the street and in the hands of friends rather than competitors. Insider trading was another charge brought to light, then immediately buried. So was the Bureau Chief after that one.

His successor had shelved the investigation. No one discussed it, no one mentioned Abbott's name, or gave the case a second thought—except for Wesley. It was another lost cause to him. He obsessed over the documents unearthed in the FBI records rooms. He met up with various witnesses. Each one pulled him deeper into the web of illicit activities that surrounded Abbott's day-to-day operations.

Machinery was missing—technology proprietary to Abbott's firm no one knew anything about, yet found interesting enough to mention. There were processors working faster than anything on the open market, computers the size of a briefcase instead of the ones that filled entire rooms: impossible advancements kept under wraps and off the books.

"You found it?" Falk asked.

No one knew where the equipment was being stored, however, not until a delivery truck was spotted in downtown Bethesda. It was parked outside a deserted warehouse, the owner part of an intricate web of shell companies that all seemed rooted in Abbott's name.

"Elm near Arlington," Wesley said. "My source thinks Abbott's been living in the place. No one's seen him for days."

"The goods and the crook in one place?" Falk exclaimed with a smile. He clapped his hands. "What are we waiting for?"

The answer to that question was obvious. Wesley's work wasn't enough to take up the ladder, and he had done everything without proper authorization. No supervisor would approve further investigation, let alone get a judge to sign off on a warrant for surveillance. There was only a young agent's due diligence and gut instinct.

"Falk..."

"Don't start again, Wes," Falk said. He leaned on the corner of the desk. His blue eyes swept over Wesley, locking him in his chair. "Abbott is a crook, and possibly a danger to everyone in the area, with the equipment he's stockpiling in that warehouse."

"We have no idea—"

"That's the point," Falk said, cutting through his argument. "No one does. I don't know a computer from a toaster oven, and probably never will. But something is off about what Tyler Abbott is doing, and no one—not this office or any other in the state—is going to do anything about it because of who he is, and who he writes his monthly donation checks to. I'm right about this. I can feel it."

"So can I," Wesley admitted. He let out a long breath and fell back in his chair. "Something is happening out there in the world, isn't it? Something no one wants us to see."

"Whoever they are, they don't get to decide that for us." Falk shuffled into his black trench coat and slipped on his fedora. His glasses caught the light from Wesley's desk, and the blue eyes behind them vanished for a second. "If no one else will do anything, it's up to us."

Wesley shook his head. "You're a terrible friend, you know that?"

"Me?" Falk said with a scoff.

"I heard about what happened with Perrin yesterday," Wesley said. "The whole damn building heard how you brought him in. I can still see the bullet hole in the sleeve of your coat. What were you thinking?"

"I was just doing my job," Falk said. "Like I am trying to do right now."

"You're reckless, and it's going to bite you in the ass one of these days."

"Not today." Falk tipped his hat at the junior agent, then

started for the door. "Now, are you coming or not?"

Rain poured down from thick gray clouds. It beat against the brick of the warehouse; the heavy flow coated everything, including Wesley's fingers. Gusts of wind caused his lock pick to slip from his grasp several times, the metal clanging much too loudly for his tastes against the pavement.

Out front, the delivery truck sat empty. The lack of windows made it impossible to peer inside the warehouse for any confirmation of what lay within. The silence of the entire area unnerved Wesley. So did the ticking of his watch and the clamoring of thunder in the distance. He needed to get inside the warehouse, and learn what Abbott was hiding before someone noticed him snooping.

"You pick that lock yet?" Falk asked. He paced the length of the building. The soles of his shoes pattered along the ground in tune with the rain. The rain coated his glasses in thin streaks. Cooler temperatures caused the thick lenses to fog up.

Wesley huffed after dropping the pick again. "You want to give it a crack, smartass?"

Falk kept his gaze on the empty street, scanning from one end of the block to the other. "What I want is to get out of the rain. I can barely see anything through these lenses. Damn glasses." He took them off to clean them on his tie. The effort only smeared the lenses more.

"I almost have it," Wesley said. "Just keep watch for another minute until…" A loud click rang out, and the door to the warehouse lifted from the frame. "There."

Before Wesley could grab hold of the handle, a gust of wind swept the door open. The metal slab crashed against the back of the frame. The sound boomed through the street and deep within the warehouse. Falk pushed past Wesley to snatch the metal before it could happen again.

"Real subtle," Falk said. "Nervous, Wes?"

Wesley stepped inside, and the pair forced the door shut against the raging wind. Darkness consumed them. "As nervous as you are calm, Falk. It's a little disconcerting."

"I've got you watching my back, don't I?" Falk replied with a smirk. "Now come on, Wes, let's go stop a bad guy."

"Hold up a second," Wesley said, catching his partner by the sleeve. "We don't know what he's building in here."

That was the reason for his nerves. For all his investigating, for all the questions asked, and the documents found in his search, there had been little in the way of answers. They came to find some, but that didn't mean they were right to do so.

That was the problem with working outside the mandate of the FBI. There was no safety net. If they were caught, their careers were over. Any chance at helping people would be gone, and the opportunity would never come again. Not for Wesley, who loved the job for that reason almost as much as he did the questions his work raised.

Falk nodded. "Whatever it is can't be good. For anyone."

"I don't disagree," Wesley said. "Just be careful."

Falk's teeth shone in the darkness. "You know me, Wes."

"That's why I said it." They started down a long hall. Boxes lined both walls. A bright light filled the center chamber of the warehouse at the end of the corridor. "I brought you into this."

"And I'm going to finish it," Falk said. "There's more out there than we know. I aim to find it."

"At the risk of your future."

Falk stopped, holding up Wesley. "You need to live in the moment, my friend. You'll figure that out, eventually."

They took each step slowly. It gave their eyes time to adjust to the growing light in the next room. When they reached the end of the corridor, their government-issued sidearms were in hand, and both were ready for anything… or so they thought.

The room stood three stories high, with landings overlooking the space from above on all sides. Cords ran from the center in every direction. Power funneled through half a dozen generators, all humming at full capacity. Computers ran off the power, stationed along three tables butted up against each other. Control consoles were positioned before the large monitors, their readings indecipherable for the pair of federal agents.

Every piece of equipment connected to a free-standing archway in the middle of the room. Stray circuits snapped, electricity sparked along the outer edge of the arch, with circuits wrapped in tight formation throughout.

Abbott stood with his back to them. He ran from monitor to console and back again in a frenzy. The sight of the man was enough to send Falk deeper into the room before Wesley was ready to act.

"Federal agents!" Falk bellowed over the crackling of power in the room. "Don't move!"

Abbott startled at their arrival. His hand fell from the controls. The look of surprise on his face turned to disgust, and his attention returned to his work. "Not now."

"Step away from the consoles, Abbott," Falk said. Wesley maintained his position near the hall. He didn't know what was happening, what they had interrupted, but every time he inched forward, there was another crackling of energy from the arch.

Falk clearly had no such concern. He pushed ahead for Abbott. "It's over!"

"It's just beginning, you fools," Abbott said. He threw a switch on the console. Light swirled around the arch. Two generators sparked from the draw, but kept humming louder and louder. "Don't you see? You're too late."

The light pooled from the machinery surrounding the gaping hole in its center. Then it darkened. The room on the other side of the arch disappeared behind a thick wall of black. Then color returned and shimmered like ripples in a pond of water.

"What the hell is that?" Wesley asked.

Abbott threw his hands into the air in triumph. "I've done it! They said I was insane, that my calculations lacked all rational thought. Dullards, all. If they could only witness this. A window into the future!"

"What?" Falk recoiled from the raving scientist. He glanced at Wesley, then back to the opening door in the center of the archway.

The image came into focus. In the haze, Wesley made out the Dentzel Carousel. The horses were on fire, the canopy scorched by the rising flames.

"Falk..." Wesley pointed to the portal. "That's Glen Echo Park."

Abbott's laughter filled the room. "I've cracked the fourth dimension!"

Falk refused to look any further. He turned toward Abbott, weapon raised. "I'm going to crack your skull if you don't turn it off. Now."

Shadows flitted through the portal. Figures shifted into view within the image. They ran in the background. Wesley took a step closer. Their cries were getting louder.

"Falk…" Wesley said, but his voice was lost to the humming of the generators.

"Stay back," Abbott said. He blocked Falk from the consoles. "Don't try to take this from me."

"I'm shutting it down," Falk said. He pushed Abbott aside and grabbed the closest lever. He pulled it down, and the power ebbed. Even with the connection dimmed, the portal remained.

"You lack my vision!" Abbott rushed at Falk. The experienced agent was ready and decked the mad scientist across the cheek. Abbott staggered back into the console. Lights flared and buttons depressed from the impact. Electricity sparked, the swirling of energy around the portal suddenly spiking uncontrollably.

"What have you done?" Abbott cried.

Lightning flew from the portal. Streaking in beams of purple, it snapped from the window to the future in all directions. The second floor landing caught fire from the initial impact. One console exploded in a fury from another strike.

Wesley retreated from the room. The view of the portal faded; the image within the arch obscured as more lightning escaped the confines. Abbott tried to correct the issue, his manic movements lost to the chaos. Falk was more concerned about Wesley. He reached out for his friend to shield him from the stray bolts of purple light.

"Wesley, stay back!" Falk yelled. "I'll—"

A bolt caught Falk in the back. His scream echoed in the warehouse, then fell silent as he vanished from sight.

"FALK!"

The portal closed. Power faded and the humming of the generators silenced. Wesley looked around for some sign of his friend, some indication of the man's presence in the warehouse. Only Abbott remained, still at work at the controls of his machine.

"Bring him back!" Wesley shouted. He leveled his weapon at the man. "Do it now!"

"I can't," Abbott replied in defiance. "I have no idea what he did. What he made me do in his ignorance."

"I said, bring him back!"

Wesley slammed his fist across the man's face. Abbott fell to the floor. Wesley took aim when he tried to stand. Fear caused the scientist to cringe, his hands raised in defense.

"I don't know how to help him," Abbott said.

Wesley didn't want to hear it. There was no way to trust the man, no way to believe a single claim spoken. Instead, Wesley set to work at the consoles. He pressed random buttons and pulled switches. The generators sparked up again, the power thrumming through the chamber.

"What are you doing?"

"Stay down, Abbott," Wesley said. His finger was tight against the trigger. He kept his eyes locked on the portal, though. "You're under arrest. I'll see you rot for this. Joshua Falk was a good man and you—"

The swirling energy surrounding the arch pooled in the center. A portal opened, the same as before, though the image was a deep red and the carousel was nothing but ashes in the background.

"How did you—" Abbott's question fell silent.

"I don't know. I..."

A figure stepped out from the portal. Lightning followed him like chains from the center of the window to the future. The figure stood before them with red eyes aglow. Sharp teeth filled his mouth. Long fingernails had grown into claws on both hands. This was no man at all. It growled at them, with dead eyes locked on Wesley.

"This wasn't you, Agent." Abbott joined Wesley at the console. "But if you don't allow me to fix this, I have a feeling we'll both soon follow your lost agent."

CHAPTER FOURTEEN

By the time they pulled into the retirement home parking lot, the sun was in decline. Wintry winds blanketed the area, shearing along the side of the car as Morgan brought it to a halt outside the door to the building.

"What are we doing back here?" Wesley glanced around in confusion. He had spent most of the ride telling his story. Questions had been asked by the agents, but the effort had been more to distract Wesley rather than heed his words.

Ben had trouble knowing where to start after hearing Wesley's tale. A quantum manipulator in 1972? Impossible didn't begin to describe such a situation. Not only that, but there were the non-answers included in Wesley's telling. Like what happened to his partner? How was Joshua Falk lost? Too many unanswered threads remained, but the most telling for both Ben and Morgan were the lack of connections to the death of Percival Jenkins.

"Mr. Fuller, it's just..." Morgan stopped. She let out a long breath, unsure how to proceed.

Ben didn't have that problem. "We have this covered, Wesley."

"Have this covered?" Disgust filled his voice. "The Jenkins kid was killed downtown, just outside the warehouse where Falk was taken. We should be there. Not here. Not at this damn place again. Didn't you hear a word I said?"

"We heard you, Mr. Fuller, but—"

Wesley raised his finger to Morgan. "And knock off the Mr. Fuller crap. It isn't some sign of respect. It's the exact opposite of that."

"Wes," Ben started. "We're going to look into the Jenkins case."

"We're heading there right—"

"As soon as we can," Ben finished, ignoring Morgan's words. He caught her wince the second they slipped out.

Wesley shook his head. "You don't believe me."

"That's not it." Morgan reached for him in the passenger seat. Wesley jolted back in revulsion. He grabbed for the handle and opened the door.

Ben leaned forward from the back of the car. "I said—"

"I heard what you said," Wesley snapped. He unbuckled his belt before exiting the car. "I've heard the same from dozens like you. Hell, I used to say the same damn thing when I wanted to do anything to get away from some crackpot."

"No one is calling you a crackpot," Morgan said.

"No," Wesley said. The wind slammed into him, and he held tight to the side of the car. "You're ignoring the situation I brought to you. Ignoring your duty as DSA agents."

"There's nothing there, Wesley," Ben shouted over the wind. "A fluke animal attack doesn't make a conspiracy. You don't know Percival Jenkins is connected to a fifty-year-old crime in the slightest. There's nothing to suggest a monster, or time travel, or any of it."

Wesley ran his hand over his face. "I can't believe I'm hearing this. What a waste of time. I never should have reached out."

"Wesley, that's not—"

"Agent Fuller," Wesley interrupted. "It used to be Agent Fuller. I don't need your pity or your help. Not anymore. He's coming for me, and when he does, I'll be ready."

The door slammed shut. Wesley moved for the front door. Morgan and Ben stayed in the car. A deep glare burrowed through Ben from the woman behind the wheel.

"What the hell was that?"

"I…" Ben sighed and fell back against the seat. "That's not how I wanted it to go."

"No?" Morgan asked. "Sure as hell sounded like it did. You didn't even give the man a chance. You, Mr. I Believe in Everything."

"There's nothing here, Morgan," Ben replied.

"Except a dead man," Morgan said. "A murder victim."

"Local PD can handle it. Don't you think we have bigger priorities right now?"

Morgan shook her head. "So we should just ignore everything else going on in the world?"

Ben shrugged his shoulders. "What was I supposed to say? Should I have lied to him? Pussyfooted around it to appease an old man who shouldn't be anywhere near this line of work any longer?"

Morgan turned off the engine, then removed her belt. She opened the car door. Before heading out, her eyes cut through Ben from the rearview mirror. "Or we could have believed him, Ben."

Ben ran his hands through his hair. He took a sharp breath, then slammed his hands down on his legs. "Dammit."

By the time he slipped from the back seat of the car, Morgan was at the front door. He raced after her, stopping her inside the reception area of the retirement home.

"What are you doing, Morgan?"

"What you usually do," she shot back at him. "Wesley isn't some random kook. He was a DSA agent."

"Fifty years ago!"

"There isn't some limit to your usefulness, Ben," Morgan said. "All your experiences don't suddenly disappear just because you gain a few wrinkles or you need a cane to help you walk."

"You think this is ageism?" Ben huffed. "That's absurd."

"Not from the way you were talking to him." Morgan led them deeper into the home. "Look. I get your concerns. I share most of them. But brushing off a man because he's retired is out of line."

"I didn't do that," Ben remarked. "Not in the least."

"We should talk to him. He could help us."

"With what?" Ben asked. "We're talking about time travel and monster men from the future. Why are you even entertaining this? You, of all people—"

Morgan stopped at the front desk. A nurse looked up from her station to greet them. "Wesley Fuller just walked by. I was hoping we could see him again."

"I can—"

"Morgan..."

She refused to turn toward him. Her fingers tapped impatiently along the edge of the desk until the nurse lowered her phone.

"I'm sorry," she said. "He doesn't seem to want company at the moment."

"If I could just—"

The nurse cringed. "Honestly, his language was much worse than that. What did you say to him?"

Morgan shot a glare at Ben. "Oh, so this is my fault?" No answer was needed. Morgan started back to the door, leaving Ben and the nurse alone at the counter. "She thinks it's my fault."

"Is it?"

"Usually." Ben shook his head. "No. Always."

He moved to follow his partner, only to find her in the middle of the reception area. A television was broadcasting the nightly news, the report listed for downtown Bethesda where it showed a body being covered at a crime scene.

"What is it?" Ben asked, though he knew the answer.

"Animal attack," Morgan said without looking at him. "There's been another murder."

CHAPTER FIFTEEN

Zac hated the job. Scrapping off leftovers into the trash, then scrubbing until his hands were raw, he finished another set of dishes before sending them off to the drying rack. There were no machines to take on the tasks. The owner never trusted them and always preferred the human element.

Zac didn't feel particularly human during his shift. More than anything, there was the very real contempt that his entire life was a fabrication—a falsehood created in his mind.

How had it come to this?

The question was one of many at the top of his list. The internal document appeared to grow with each endless shift. Thinking was all that was left to him, Zac's spiraling thoughts nothing more than a reminder of his failures.

He had taken the job to keep himself afloat. Sure, he had plenty of funds in his account—his shared account with Claire— but dipping in meant stealing from his wife and son. Claire's teaching position had never been enough to pay the bills. Zac had always taken care of the rest. He couldn't abandon them now, at least not monetarily. If struggling through menial tasks gave some semblance of financial security to Claire and his son, then it was all worth it in his eyes.

Zac checked the time. Eight hours had passed in the blink of an eye. Between the dishes, and the subsequent washing of the floor, Zac lost track of another day. It happened more and more. Time slipped away from him even with his eyes fully open.

Now it was late afternoon. He needed to call her. Being apart was one thing, wanting to give her the space she desired a necessity. Zac, however, needed to hear his wife's voice just for a moment. It was all that mattered to him — if only it had mattered when it counted.

"Hey," Zac called from the sink. A portly man in a stained apron stopped at the far end of the kitchen. He threw Zac a quizzical look, one Zac had seen every day from Julian Neves since taking the position. "I need a break, Julian."

"You were late."

Zac groaned. "And I promised to cover Gerri's shift for you tonight. Come on."

Julian's hands balled into fists. "Make it quick. Dinner crowd will be picking up any minute."

The corpulent manager left the kitchen without another word, or without seeing Zac nod his acceptance of the situation. Zac waited for him to depart before wiping his hands clean on the towel hanging from the sink. He slipped off his own stained and soaked apron, then started for the dining area.

The door flapped closed behind him. His entrance won the stares of all four patrons currently enjoying their meals, and the two old men who basically lived at the counter. Zac rolled his eyes. He wondered what Julian would say when an actual crowd showed up. Not that it was a likely scenario with the anger and contempt most of the staff held for humanity.

A payphone was attached to the wall between the restrooms in the back of the dining room. No patrons sat in the area. Most stayed by the windows and the front doors to give the illusion of a crowd from the street. Zac tucked near the device and lifted the receiver to his ear.

The phone chirped twice before Claire's voice filled the speaker. "Hello?"

Zac remained silent for a moment. His heart fluttered at the sound of her voice. The sensation carried with it the years they spent together, from late nights in the dorm to the early days in the house sleeping on the floor while they saved for a decent bed.

"Hello?" she asked again.

Zac's eyes widened. "C... Claire. It's me."

"Zac." Her tone was solemn, not the excitement she once shared when he came home from work. Only sadness remained. "You shouldn't call here anymore, Zac. I told you that last time. Please respect that decision."

"I know," Zac replied, biting his lower lip. "I do, I really do. It's been a few days, and I was worried about you and Alex."

"You don't..." Claire trailed off. He could almost hear the tears falling. It caused his vision to blur, and his head lowered to the side of the payphone. "You don't have to worry about us anymore. It's too late for that."

"What does that mean?" Zac's grip tightened to the receiver. "I know I screwed up, Claire, but I never stopped loving you. You have to believe that."

"I don't," she said, her voice loud and booming in his ear. "Zac, I... I reached out to an attorney. She's drawing up divorce papers."

"What?" Zac nearly dropped the phone. His chest hurt. Had his affair with Morgan truly robbed them of a second chance? No, he knew better. The damage had been done long before the affair. It had come from days spent away at work, putting every ounce of energy into propping up a secret government organization rather than building a life with his wife and son. He had made this bed every morning he'd raced away from the responsibilities of adulthood for the prestige of helping his country. "Claire, I... You can't."

"It's too—"

"Modine!" Julian bellowed. Zac jumped; his right side slammed into the wall at the sound of the man's voice. Julian pointed to the kitchen. "Get your ass back in there! Dishes are piling up!"

"One... I need a minute here."

"Hang up the phone and get to work."

"Zac?" Claire asked, concern in her voice.

Zac covered up the receiver, his swollen eyes staring down his superior. "One. Minute."

Julian threw up a finger—Zac wasn't sure which one—then stomped his way toward the kitchen. No dishes were piling up. It was a power play, one Zac had seen hundreds of times at the DSA. It was one he had cowered down to on more than one occasion.

Zac took a deep breath to calm his nerves before removing his fingers from the speaker. "Claire?"

"I... I'm here."

"Listen. Please listen," Zac said. "I know I messed this up. I can't take back what I've done. But I'm trying. I'm trying to be a better man, a better person for you. I am—"

"Zac..."

Zac closed his eyes. "Julian, I swear to God, I just need a minute to—"

He turned around, but found no sign of Julian. No one was in view.

"Zac?" Claire said. "Who are you talking to? I didn't hear anyone else talking."

"You didn't?" The voice had said his name. Just like at the Vroman's earlier. *What the hell is happening to me?*

"Zac, I have to go."

"Claire, wait, I—"

"I can't do this anymore, Zac," Claire continued. "I have to do what's best for Alex. Don't call here again. Please."

"Claire..." The line went dead. "Claire!"

He slammed the receiver down. His head rested against the cool metal of the payphone. Dishes waited for him, another night of menial tasks ahead of him. The life he earned through his choices.

CHAPTER SIXTEEN

Silence carried them to the crime scene. Cordons were set up at neighboring intersections. The entire block was cut off from the city, like a microcosm of law and order. Forensics rushed to and from the scene, coordinating with other officials to move as efficiently as possible.

Officers working the cordon helped escort those that needed access to the area toward a waiting zone to have their issues addressed. There were businesses to consider, apartments on the left-hand side of the street and above the shops dominating the right.

Morgan parked the car outside the cordon. It was in front of a fire hydrant, but after circling the block three times, she grew sick of searching. She didn't know what to say to Ben anymore. The way he had shunted Wesley off, blown off the man's claims, wasn't like him. She hadn't known Ben very long, but they had grown to respect each other during that time. She'd understood his almost obsessive need to help people. To see him go against that impulse, that defined trait so embedded within his heart, worried Morgan.

Rather than tip back into another argument, Morgan said nothing. She turned off the engine, reached for the handle, and opened the door. The crisp evening air met her with a fierce gust of wind. It blew her hair over her eyes. When she could see clearly again, Ben was waiting for her in front of the car.

"What are you doing?"

Ben shot her a confused look. "Going to the crime scene?" He turned and pointed at the flashing lights throughout the area. "The one you, for some unknown reason, think might be connected with Wesley? Did you forget to take your crazy pills, Morgan?"

The sarcasm was the worst part. He claimed it to be a diffusing mechanism when it came to conflict. Since his return to the team, the only thing his sarcasm had diffused was his ability to hold a conversation.

"Why don't you wait here?" Morgan asked. "I can ask a few questions on my own."

"Without my wit and charm to ably assist? Perish the thought."

Morgan cut him off from the nearest cordon. "It's fine, Ben, really. You've been pushing yourself. Take a few minutes."

Ben took a step back, his hand to his chin. "Is this because of what I said to Wesley before? Look, I went too far, I know. But he needed—"

"It's not about that," she said much too quickly, and they both realized it. That was only part of it, yet she held the rest back. This wasn't the time or place for the conversation. "Take a break, partner."

"I'm not going to argue with you," Ben said, hands in the air.

"Good, I—"

Ben pushed ahead of her, his badge already in place when he reached the cordon. "I'm just going to ignore you."

The officer barring the gate let him through. Morgan stared as Ben stuck his tongue out at her before continuing deeper into the scene. She shoved her hands in her pocket to get her own badge. A long sigh escaped her lips.

"Of course you are."

She followed Ben into the maw of the crime scene. Cars blocked the area to keep the media coverage at bay. Personnel took care of the rest, and the pair waded through them to find the heart of the matter.

Spatter markers were laid out along the walkway. The body rested in the center, covered by a thin sheet to keep the dead out of sight as much as possible. Spotlights lit up the sidewalk, great beams of illumination against the growing gloom of night. It wasn't the sight of the body that stopped Morgan in her tracks and caused Ben to join her; it was where the body was found: in front of the post office.

"Still think this has nothing to do with Wesley?" Her sudden shock drew the attention of those at the scene, including a fierce woman in flats and a baseball cap. Her badge glistened under the spotlight, the word DETECTIVE clear for all to read.

Ben leaned close. "Ever hear of a coincidence?"

"Not in this line of work," Morgan replied, then left him — and his anger — behind.

"Who are you supposed to be now?" the detective asked when they approached.

Morgan showed off her badge, the move quick and concise. "Agents Dunleavy and Riley."

The woman groaned in disgust. She rubbed at her brow. "The damn media have turned this into a field day. I spend more time working the cordon than the crime scene."

The pair waited for her to calm down. They had been through this with liaisons before. Working with others was nothing more than a giant pain in the ass to most of the planet, so they understood the detective's reticence to share.

Eventually, she let the frustration go with a long breath, then extended her hand to welcome them. "Debra Combes. Detective."

Morgan took the hand and shook. Stepping back, Ben shifted in front of her. He held out his hand. "Please to meet — "

Combes turned away, the disgust clearly back at the distraction. Rounding the body, she waved them over. "Let's get this over with already."

Ben lowered the hand. "Guess I should have stayed in the car."

"Someday you'll listen to me."

Both put on a pair of gloves. Morgan moved for the body. That was her area of expertise. Ben remained on the perimeter, circling the scene; his own unique talent for taking in details had always proven useful for their work.

Morgan lifted the sheet. She had become used to horrible deaths over the years, especially having seen her fair share of deformities in the Middle East. Still, the state of the deceased nearly caused her to gag.

He was male, but beyond that, there was little she could discern from her initial inspection. There was too much damage to the body. Claw marks made identification a mess. The man's face was sliced open in several long drags. The same held true for his midsection, as if he'd been gutted by his attacker. He was more raw hamburger than man.

"There's no real reason for the feds to be involved," Combes said, reading Morgan's reaction. "Looks like another animal attack."

"Like the Jenkins scene?"

"You're well-informed," Combes replied. It was a dig at her, to be sure. The news continued to replay the grisly death. There were plenty of opportunities for Morgan to find out more about the details. However, her information came from a specific source.

"We had some help," Morgan said. "A former agent named Fuller."

Combes' eyes sparked at the name. "Wes called you in? Must be serious, then."

"You know him?" The surprise in Ben's voice matched the detective's.

Combes shifted closer to the building and away from the body. Morgan and Ben followed, which cleared the way for a pair of analysts to continue their work. "Wes comes down to the station a couple times each month. Always offers tips on active investigations. Insights no one else had when it comes to the case. The department thinks he's a loon."

Ben grinned at the comment. Morgan raised a finger to keep him silent on the subject, then focused on the detective once more. "Do you think that?"

Combes sighed. Her hands fell to her hips, and she shook her head. "No. He's intense and not always tactful, but like him or not, Wes Fuller is almost always right. About every damn thing."

Morgan threw Ben a glare. He closed his eyes and shuffled back to the scene.

"Not what you wanted to hear?" Combes asked.

"No," Morgan said. "It's not that. I mean—"

Combes moved back to the scene. "He's a good egg, Agent. Trust his judgment. I do. Now what's he say about this mess?"

Morgan joined her. The pair stared at the deceased. "He doesn't believe it's an animal attack, for one."

"Not a—" Combes' head dropped, a curse on her lips. "How does he do that?"

"Wait," Morgan said. "You knew? But you said—"

"I don't know you," Combes shot back. "And I'm still waiting for DNA on Mr. Linden here. Particulates collected in the scratches along his neck. This is almost too extreme for an animal attack. Too thought out about where to make the strikes to make my job that much more difficult. Like the killer was trying to obscure something about the victim. Which means this man was targeted for a reason. Which means *someone* did this, not something."

Ben stood at the brick wall leading to the post office branch. His fingers grazed the eagle symbol carved into the single red block at the center of the wall. His head fell low. When he turned back, Morgan was waiting. Their shared silence spoke volumes. So did his nod of agreement.

"Thank you, Detective," Morgan said. "If you don't mind, we'd—"

"I do," Combes answered. Both needed the body for analysis. Both needed evidence to pursue their theories. Combes wasn't having it. "Sorry, but I'm not playing the jurisdiction game in front of a fresh victim. My team has this covered and will send you the details."

Morgan wanted to push for access. Combes didn't give her the chance.

"Look," the detective continued. "I get it. We're all doing the job. Catching the monster before another body comes along."

"Glad you see it that way."

Combes grabbed her notebook and pulled out a preliminary sheet. Along the side margin, she jotted something down, then passed it over to Morgan. "Here."

"What's this?"

"Linden's information," Combes said. "What we have so far. I'll send over preliminaries in the hour."

"This note?" Morgan pointed to the scribble. "There's an address here."

Combes nodded. "Percival Jenkins' apartment. If you want somewhere to start, may as well be with victim number one."

"Thank you for this."

"Sounds like you should be thanking Wes Fuller," Combes said. "I'll be sure to do the same when this is over."

CHAPTER SEVENTEEN

The hunter continued to falter in his mission. Two had fallen by his hand. Just the sight of a similar-looking man had been enough to drive his bloodlust out of control. Neither, however, had been the target the hunter had desired. Neither had provided him with the key to his escape from this time and this place.

Everything about the world overwhelmed the hunter. The sights and smells bombarded every synapse. The sound alone was enough to drive him mad from prolonged exposure.

Not only was the world consumed by the sounds of technology, even the background contained a steady stream of radio waves. They were imperceptible to the normal human, but not to someone genetically altered like the hunter. How humanity survived in such utter chaos astounded him on every level. Since his arrival back in the world, he had found no peace and no calm to collect his thoughts.

The hunter had believed his task a simple matter: eliminate the target known as Wesley Fuller. Yet, ever since his return, the hunter had been plagued by his own ineptitude. He had been trained—programmed with the talents of his betters—yet failed twice.

The second death had been a matter of circumstance and surprise. He had been tracking the scent of his prey through the streets of Bethesda. His appearance made an outright journey impossible. He wore the trench coat of his first victim to blend in with the throng of people in the downtown area, while also using the growing shadows of the evening to stay out of full view. He preferred the dark.

The scent collected from the first murder had brought the

hunter to a government facility in the city's heart. The sign out-side listed the place as a post office, though the name held no meaning for the hunter. Such trivialities no longer existed in his time. Life was more basic—more instinctual and true. His own personal beliefs mattered little, however, in the hunt. That his target had frequented the area recently spurred him closer and closer to the structure until he was outside the front door.

That was when it had happened. A man had exited the build-ing at the moment of the hunter's arrival. He had worn the same tan trench coat and carried the same matted down, dusty hair of the target the hunter had seen so long ago. Without hesitation, without a growl of righteous fury, the hunter struck the man in the trench coat down.

His desire to return home had outweighed his common sense. The hunter grew sick of the world around him, dreaming of nothing more than slaughtering Fuller and completing his mission. Yet, in his haste, all the hunter had done was cause the death of another innocent.

The hunter had taken to the shadows quickly. His kill had been too public, and onlookers caught sight of the dead man al-most immediately. The police had arrived less than fifteen minutes later. The hunter had originally thought to use the scene as a distraction, to escape and take up the search for his target once more.

Then he'd thought better. With the amount of attention the dead man had pulled, there was the chance of drawing his target to him. And he had, in a way.

The two latecomers to the scene were somehow connected with his target. The scent of Fuller was upon them; they had been in his presence.

They were the key.

The hunter nearly salivated at the discovery. It took every ounce of his willpower to contain himself. He waited for the pair of officials to slip away from the crowd. The hunter stayed in the shadows to give them space, but kept the unseen leash short for fear of losing the trail and the scent of his target.

The scent was different, aged somehow from what he re-membered of their first encounter. It was no wonder his search-ing ended with two failures and no constructive leads to follow. Time had changed matters.

"You sure this is the right move?" the male said to his companion. He hid his anger well from her, but to the hunter at their backs, it was all too apparent. The agents were together, yet separate in their priorities. It led to them being distracted enough for the hunter to push through them for the open street beyond.

"Hey, watch it!" the woman protested. The hunter made no motion of apology. He merely tucked his head lower, savoring the pair's proximity to his target. They had come from Fuller and the trail lit up before the hunter. He could still hear the woman's frustration when he reached the end of the block. "Jerk."

"Want me to drive?" the man asked.

"Get in the car, Riley."

The hunter waited at the corner for them to depart. If they turned right, he would follow, but they went left, away from the trail ablaze in his senses.

Perfect.

His patience paid off. There would be no defense for his target, and no more chances. The hunter, no longer confined to the human population occupying the crime scene, raced through the downtown area. Most only witnessed the world on a superficial level, through eyes that never truly saw everything in their path. The hunter, however, perceived spectra just tucked out of range. His every sense connected with the scent of his target, locking onto the man even from a great distance.

His search led him down blocks and through residential and business districts. Rushing steps never grew weary, and the connection never wavered in the time spent traveling. All came to fruition when, at last, the hunter came to a halt outside a large complex on a quiet street.

The wind blew harder; each gust carried the scent to him. The target was inside, a resident in a place for the aged. Time had indeed shifted matters. The ending, however, would come the same way it should have long ago.

The hunter tasted his revenge on the air. The completion of his mission had finally arrived.

CHAPTER EIGHTEEN

Zac picked at his dinner. It had been waiting for him when he walked in the door, along with his host. Nancy had long since finished her meal, yet sat patiently at his arrival despite the late hour and the lack of call from him about extending his shift.

Micah sat between them, his homework on the table and his headphones turned up to the max. He rolled his eyes with each strained glare from his mother—a look Zac tried his best not to reciprocate.

The exhausted dishwasher sat in his chair and used his fork to probe the lukewarm contents of the chicken and mixed vegetable meal gratefully provided by the matronly woman at the far end of the table.

"It's so nice to have a man back in the house," Nancy said, elbows propped at the edge of the table and hands pressed tight to her cheeks. "Isn't that right, Micah?"

The boy of seventeen kept his head down and his eyes focused on the math worksheet.

"Micah?" Nancy shouted. Zac's fingers slipped on the fork, barely able to catch the utensil before it crashed against the side of the plate. Peas rolled loose from the effort, and he sought to collect them. Nancy pounded on the table next to her son, who flinched back. He threw the headphones off, letting them settle along his neck.

"What?" he asked in confusion. "What did I do?"

"I said, isn't it nice to have a man back in the house?"

"Seriously?"

Nancy's eyes thinned. She maintained her smile. "Micah…"

"Yeah, Ma," Micah said. "Sure. It's great. If you can call him that."

Nancy said nothing, the comment clearly ignored as her attention returned to Zac. The quiet tenant tried to focus on his meal; his stomach churned with each minuscule bite.

It wasn't that the meal was terrible. During his tenure at the DSA, home-cooked meals had been a rare treat. There had always been another briefing to prepare, or an operation to oversee. Takeout had been his go-to move for food.

More than his discomfort at being in the room with his hosts, Zac's stomach refused to settle. Each bite drove a sharp pain into his gut. He did his best to work through the issue. He had always done well at swallowing his own personal problems for the betterment of others.

Nancy's probing questions made it more difficult. "Is the chicken all right? Not too dry?"

"It's delicious," Zac replied between bites. "It's—"

"Barbecue sauce really brings out the flavor." She was on her feet before he finished answering. The bottle settled at his side, and she loomed above him with a beaming smile on her face. "Try some."

Zac quietly opened the bottle and poured out the contents on his plate. He dipped a piece of the tasteless meat into the sauce, then shoved it in his mouth. His stomach gurgled in an uproar. He muted its discontent with a satisfied moan that pleased his host.

"Good," she said. Her hand snatched his and squeezed. "I'm glad you like it."

Her hand was warm to the touch. Zac pulled away. Grabbing his napkin in a quick movement, he cleaned up his lips to hide from her sudden shock.

"Everything all right?"

He knew the answer to that question. It was one of the few Zac could find plenty to talk about. No way in hell was everything all right. Nancy's touch brought it home for him.

Claire.

His wife's words on the phone earlier stuck with him. A divorce attorney had been brought in, his affair had destroyed his marriage. He thought there would be more time. The idea of giving her space had been to allow for his own chance to put his life in order, to be a better person who Claire would want to take back. Space had been the death knell, it seemed.

Nancy was still staring at him. Zac cleared his throat and offered a sad smile. "Everything is wonderful."

The matronly host pulled the adjacent chair loose and sat at his side. A soft giggle escaped her as she shifted closer to him. "It's the least I could do. You've been such a help around here, Zac. With the dryer and the computer last week, and the toaster and the coffeemaker, I swear I don't understand why I am so technologically challenged."

"Not a problem," Zac said, swallowing another small bite of vegetables. "I enjoy fixing things."

It was strange that so much had failed since his arrival. When she mentioned working around the house, it had originally been more on the physical side of things. The yard needed trimming. The living room needed a fresh coat of paint, the supplies resting and waiting in the room's corner. Yet the day after he had arrived, her computer went on the fritz. The television followed soon after. None of the incidents had been serious, and Zac had found workarounds, yet it remained curious to him.

"Well, I think you're a miracle worker."

"It was nothing, Ms. Vroman," Zac said. He lowered his fork to the side of the plate and settled the napkin over the rest of his uneaten meal.

"Nancy."

Zac nodded. "Nancy."

"Well," she said, "I wish you would reconsider staying longer."

Micah lifted his head, eyes wide in bewilderment. "What? Seriously?"

Nancy's eyes narrowed on her son. "Don't be rude, Micah."

The tension sat between them. Zac saw the wheels turning in Micah's mind. Another slam against their guest was being workshopped, no doubt. Zac stood and collected his dishes, their attention back on him at the sudden movement.

"I wish I could," Zac said. "I have responsibilities I've ignored for too long." He had intended to stay a few more weeks, but the money earned from his double shift would have to do for a bus ride back to Bethesda. He refused to let Claire go without a fight. "More things for me to fix back home."

Micah laughed. "The mysteries of life solved by the master

dishwasher. What could go wrong?"

Nancy's fists clenched at her sides. Tension ran along her shoulders. "Upstairs, young man."

"Ma?"

She pointed to the stairs. "Now!"

"Come on!" Micah pushed off the table. Gathering his schoolwork into his bag, the teenager stomped his way out of the dining room for the stairs.

Nancy waited for his bedroom door to slam before wiping at her tired eyes. "I'm sorry about him. His father had the same problem with his mouth. Should've sewn the thing shut."

Zac smiled. "He's not wrong, Nancy. I am getting pretty good at this dishwashing thing."

"I can help."

Zac shook his head. "Not after cooking the meal. I've got this."

He started for the kitchen, letting the light remain off when he entered. His head was pounding, probably from the long day. He knew the layout after the last three weeks, so the bright overhead fixtures were unnecessary. Instead, he flicked on the lone bulb resting over the sink. He wiped the uneaten contents of his meal into the trash can. His dish settled into the basin, and he turned on the hot water.

It was time to leave. Claire and Alex needed him. A quick call to Julian at the diner would make it official. That alone made the whole notion of departing worthwhile.

"*Zac...*"

Zac spun around at the sound of the voice. The darkness of the empty room surrounded him. "Who said that? Who's there?"

No reply came from the shadows. He turned back to the filling sink and the waiting dishes. His hands settled at the edge of the counter, and he closed his eyes to shake away the voice.

"Zac?"

His eyes snapped open. Nancy's hand was on his shoulder. "Zac, are you okay?"

The lights were on in the room. Water ran over the lip of the sink. "Nancy? What's going on?"

"I thought I heard you call out from the other room," Nancy said. She turned off the faucet, then opened the drain at the bottom. "I asked if you were all right, but there was no response. I didn't want to pry if you were on the phone with someone, but I started to worry. When I finally came in, you were just standing here, and the sink was overflowing."

"How?" Zac muttered. He stepped away from the sink. How had it filled so quickly? He had closed his eyes for only a second. How had Nancy gotten next to him without him noticing? "I mean, I..."

Nancy patted his back softly. "Why don't you get some rest? I'll take care of this."

Zac hesitated. He needed answers about the voice, about the time slipping away without warning. But he was so tired. "Yeah. Okay. I will."

"Feel better," she called after him as he left the room. There was concern in her voice, but it paled compared to his own, which grew by the second.

CHAPTER NINETEEN

"Take the road up here on the left."

Metcalf slowed to make the turn. She didn't bother to indicate the shift. No other cars trailed them on the road. Their travels had taken them from the massive crowds of DC to the farmlands of Maryland. By the time they'd left the busy streets and even the modest townships, the sun had set. The car's headlights were their only light, and Nixon their only guide.

Kanigher stewed in the passenger seat. This was clearly not how he wanted the day to go. Their talk of trust had ended prematurely, the matter still unresolved in both of their eyes. He wanted things to be how they were in the beginning, when it was just the two of them with Grissom navigating the political quagmire that was Washington.

Those days were gone—dead and buried, much like Grissom himself. She hadn't told Kanigher the truth about their friend. Grissom had betrayed them, and the revelation continued to haunt her every waking moment. The fact that she had been blind to his betrayal, that even with everything she now knew, she still questioned the validity of Morgan's claim. Yet, the evidence was clear. It slapped her in the face. Trust was an illusion.

"It's coming up," Nixon said, stirring her from her thoughts. "Take the drive on the right."

"Where?" Metcalf asked.

Nixon's arm shot out, his finger pointing ahead to a small inlet barely seen thanks to the thick brush that covered the road. It wasn't so much a driveway as a dirt path cut through the trees, but Metcalf took the turn.

Twisting around a bend under the shadows of the trees, they

came to a cabin in the woods. It was a ramshackle home. The shutters beat against the log construct. The place appeared empty, but they heard the motor of a generator tied to the side of the domicile.

Nixon was the first out of the car. He waved them ahead toward the front porch. "Welcome to my palace."

Kanigher grumbled audibly. The car door screeched open to drown out his frustration. Metcalf exited the vehicle and joined him along the passenger side.

"Nothing creepy about this."

"Bobby…"

"We're in the middle of nowhere," he continued. The time for holding his tongue was over, it appeared. "This has ambush written all over it."

"Why would Nixon set us up?"

"Did you see those cops before?" Kanigher asked. "They just happen to show up like they did? And what do we do? We save the guy, promising to keep him safe. Bringing him right into the thick of it. No background checks. No way to verify his damn story at all. He's playing us, Susan."

Nixon held the front door open. "I don't know how those cops found me. I take every necessary precaution to avoid situations like that."

"Yeah, right."

"Feel free to drive away, pal," Nixon snapped. "I didn't ask for this, or for you to show up in my life today. Now come in or don't. I don't care."

Nixon let the door slam behind him. Metcalf's hands fell to her hips, her head low and unable to meet the angry gaze of her colleague.

"Happy now?"

"I will be when we get back to the Bunker and forget this whole day." Kanigher moved for the car. She stepped in front of him.

"Not yet," she said. "We're not just leaving. Not without him."

"We're exposed here, Susan," Kanigher said. "You see that, don't you? There are dozens of places to ambush us out here. If he's not on the level—"

"What if he is?" she shot back. "Have you even thought for a second about that? We're outnumbered and outgunned on every level with this enemy, Bobby. I can't fight a war that way."

"So stop fighting," he said. Sad eyes caught her gaze. "Let someone else pick up where you left off."

"I can't do that. Neither can you." She started for the house. "Or maybe I don't know you as well as I thought I did."

"Susan," Kanigher called after her.

She stopped on the porch, her hand at the door. "You don't have to trust him, Bobby. But you should trust me."

"I do."

"Then give him a chance."

Kanigher's fists clenched tight at his sides. He glanced around the woods. She could tell he was taking in every shadow and every unseen threat. He was always the protector. Stepping toward the house, he removed his gun from his holster but kept it at his side.

"Bobby…"

He shook his head. "Take it or leave it. I'm not walking into anything unprepared."

"Okay," she replied. She opened the door for him. He took the lead, his pistol at the ready.

The small entryway of the home immediately split in two directions. There was a kitchen to the left, a small table against the wall. It was covered in dirty dishes. To the right, at the end of the thin corridor, was the bathroom. They took the first bend, passing a bedroom before taking another turn into the main living area.

A buzzing sound met them upon entering the room. Rolling to them on an uneven pair of what appeared to be roller-skate wheels was a sparking hunk of mechanical junk. It held a platter with a spilled glass of water on top. When it bumped into Kanigher's leg, the agent flinched away.

"What the hell?"

Nixon raced over from the other side of the room. "Jeeves gets a little enthusiastic about helping."

"Jeeves?" Metcalf asked, a smirk at the corner of her lips. Kanigher found nothing amusing about the robotic butler in the shape of the Jetson's housekeeper.

"A work in progress," Nixon admitted as he shut the half-pint helper down with the flick of a switch. He pointed to the pile of debris in the corner of the room. Dozens of spare parts occupied the floor. From sheet metal to dials and wires, the area appeared little more than a mini-warehouse. "Supplies are limited when you're trying not to attract too much attention."

"I thought he was a hacker?" Kanigher asked.

"I am," Nixon interjected. "You don't get a degree in hacking, though, do you? Robotics is a passion. Keeps the mind working."

"Yeah," Kanigher grumbled. "That's what it looks like here."

"Let it go, Bobby."

Nixon retreated for the stairs that made up the far wall. They led to a second-floor balcony that overlooked the entire space. From her position, Metcalf noticed more bedrooms on the second floor, as well as another bathroom.

Kanigher's focus wasn't on the home's layout. Pictures dominated the wall in front of the staircase. These were not the usual family-oriented images. There was no sign of the Jessup clan at holidays, or on vacation, or whatever the hell normal people did with their families. Instead, there were photos of random individuals. Each one was connected to the next through a series of tacks and string that created a web over the wall. Printed reports and newspaper articles filled the spaces between images. "What is this now?"

"This is the Trust." Nixon stepped out from the back of the cabin. Lights kicked on brighter, the generator fully warmed up. "I started monitoring chatter years ago. The stock exchange was a good place to start, I thought. It's amazing what's said in a room full of people screaming at each other every minute of the business day. Deals were drawn up. Companies merged."

Nixon pointed to one man pictured on the outer edges of the web. "A thin strand like a tech company bought out by a chief rival sends a ripple across ten countries and a dozen different industries. Look closer and you see the same names across all these little, seemingly insignificant deals. Then follow the string to another merger, impacting an entire sector of life. Drug companies. The housing market. Each leads to another deal. Then another. It paints a dangerous picture."

Kanigher threw Metcalf a thin glare. "It certainly does."

"Don't," Metcalf muttered.

Kanigher leaned close. "He's a mental patient."

"If he's wrong, sure."

"If he's right?" Kanigher said. "How the hell did he find all this?"

"By looking," Nixon interjected. "Anyone could have done it."

Metcalf turned Kanigher away from Nixon before more was said. "Bobby, if there is a shred of truth here, it could help us bring the fight to the Trust."

"The truth?" Kanigher pulled away from Metcalf for the web on the wall. "Look at these names. These connections." He pointed to a middle-aged man with an award-winning smile and perfect teeth. "This guy? This is Bryant St. James. He's a cereal mogul. Are you telling me I'm being controlled and manipulated by the guy behind Fruit Loops?"

"That's someone different," Nixon said. He grabbed his bag from the couch. Opening it up, he pulled out a tablet and set to work. His fingers danced on the screen. When silence filled the room, he glanced up at the empty stare of Kanigher and pointed to the image on the wall. "The Fruit Loops guy is someone different, I mean. Nice guy too. St. James, though, is involved in the Trust, I promise you that."

"Your promise doesn't mean—"

Metcalf stepped between them, cutting Kanigher off. "We came here, Nixon. We want to keep you safe. You can see that. Now it's your turn to prove something to us."

"Right." Nixon continued to work on the tablet. The sound of his fingers slamming against the glass of the screen caused Kanigher's teeth to grind. Nixon ignored the sound. He finished his work before tucking the tablet under his arm. He stepped over to the web. "St. James wasn't smart or quiet about his work. Cereal is where he made his millions, but he has a hand in pharmaceuticals like Jen-Pad, Shur-Rite, and more. I've found payments to law enforcement agencies. Hush money offered to the highest officials, including Donald Stallworth and Greg Sullivan."

It was a damning accusation if proven correct. Kanigher, however, continued to shake his head. "That could be for anything."

"Bobby."

"No, Susan," Kanigher said. "I didn't come to play this game.

We need concrete evidence that the Trust is real, that these people exist. St. James could be anyone. So, where is the proof, Nixon?"

"Right now?" Nixon said. "Everywhere."

Metcalf's eyes widened. "What did you do?"

Nixon showed them the screen of the tablet. Several files shot across the screen, delivered and dispersed in rapid fashion. "I just sent out my proof on the web. Each one carries my digital footprint." He tossed the tablet to Kanigher, who looked through it in sudden silence. "St. James is a Trust member, and I'll be glad to prove it to you, Agent. All you have to do is wait."

"For what?" Kanigher asked.

Nixon pointed to the clock on the wall. "To see how long it takes for them to come here and kill me."

CHAPTER TWENTY

They didn't believe him. That thought carried Wesley through the rest of his evening. It repeated during his meal, one he merely picked at. The turkey was dry and the potatoes cold. It's not like he missed much.

Still, Ben and Morgan's reaction to his tale woke Wesley to the truth of his situation. His time had long since passed. His usefulness to the world had dried up and withered on a vine of neglect. Sure, there were moments of lucidity—downright brilliance—that the local precinct accepted before going on their merry way. But they, too, were reticent to trust in the word of an old man who had turned in his badge decades earlier.

After dinner, alone at his corner table, Wesley retired for the night. He felt no need for television, or the frustrated stares of his contemporaries. Even the attendants sighed with relief when Wesley departed the common areas for the quiet of his bed. No one wanted to put up with him, and now he had a better understanding of why.

Wesley closed the door behind him. He started for the window and the comfort of his chair. It was home to him more than anywhere else in the world. He looked himself over as his ass hit the cushion.

No wonder they hadn't believed him. Stains dotted his shirt in multiple spots. A hole sat on the knee of his pants. One leg was tucked squarely in his socks, the other frayed and resting atop his shoe. His appearance resembled a homeless man more than an investigator. Ben and Morgan had been right to push him aside. There was a murder to solve. What good would it be to bring Wesley any further into matters?

Wesley stared out at the fading light of the day. He wondered when hope left him. It was something he had always carried in the field—a belief that at the end of the day he'd always done more good than bad. The mistakes remained, but so did the wonder. His time handling cases for the DSA were some of the best years of his life... and the worst.

Wesley groaned as he vacated the chair. He pulled a photo from the corner of the shelf and held it close. Opening up the back, Wesley removed the image, then set the frame where it belonged. He smiled at the man in the photo. There had been such vigor in his spirit, such immense self-importance in every act. That man—although barely able to call himself that, considering his voice cracked when approached by an attractive woman—lived his life to the fullest. That man had gumption and standards and never caved in to the prejudices of his peers.

The image unfolded beneath his fingers. He let the back half, the one he tried to hide in the frame, remain unseen for a long moment. If he so much as glanced at it, he knew what would happen. The old recriminations would return. They had held him back from a life, a successful career, and who knows how many other things. It was an earned guilt for what happened—for what he could have, and should have, prevented.

Wesley lifted the hidden portion of the photo. His eyes watered at the sight of the man standing beside his younger self. The image had been taken just days before his disappearance.

Joshua Falk wore darker colors, blending with the shadows compared to Wesley's prestigious tan trench coat. A black one to match the fedora on his head had been Falk's claim to fame. That and the thick, rounded spectacles he always wore. Looking at them straight on, one could see the sharp blue of his eyes, but if one shifted a single step to either side, they were lost behind the frames of his glasses.

"This is all my fault," Wesley said to the man in the image: the man he'd failed to save when it counted. "Even after so long, it's still my fault."

Wesley clutched tight to the image and carried it with him to his bed. He didn't bother to change his clothes. He was suddenly too weary to worry about that. His only concern centered on the young man—Percival Jenkins—dead because of him. He'd brought the monster to this place. All the blood that followed was on him.

It started with Falk.

Wesley closed his eyes with the photo resting on his chest. Thoughts of the past flashed behind his lids from his first case with the DSA.

All those years ago…

CHAPTER TWENTY-ONE
April 5th, 1972

The monster snarled at them. He wore what appeared to be a uniform — Army fatigues — though they looked unlike anything Wesley had ever seen before. A collar, adorned in blue lights, wrapped around his neck. His boots pounded against the concrete floor, stomping closer and closer with each step. Claws scratched at the open space between them, red rage in his dead eyes.

"My God," Wesley muttered.

Abbott was not as lost as Wesley. He pushed the agent aside. "Move, you fool!"

The scientist set to work on the console. He pulled the plug on each relay, dropped every lever to disrupt the power supply currently being channeled into the portal that somehow brought the monster to their world.

No, their time. According to Abbott, the thing was from the future. How such a monster could be possible escaped Wesley. Almost everything did; the loss of Falk still screamed in his mind. His partner was gone, wiped from existence in a single burst of light. In his place stood a creature pulled from the depths of hell.

"Shoot it!" Abbott screamed from the controls. Power faded from the archway, yet the portal remained. So did the threat in the room. "Kill the damn thing already!"

"I—" Wesley hesitated. He lifted his sidearm, but couldn't fire. He couldn't take the chance. Falk disappeared, and an instant later, the monster arrived. Was there a chance he was his friend and colleague? There were no signs in the manner of dress, in the cold, dead eyes of the monster. Yet something held Wesley back, allowing the beast to reach the console.

Abbott pulled back at the last second. Claws sliced through delicate wiring. Sparks erupted from the damaged circuitry. Instead of winding down, the generators revved up. Power flowed faster through the mechanisms and leaked out of the exposed core.

The monster jumped over the table, landing before a frightened and reeling Abbott. The scientist tried to escape. He tripped over the wiring in his haste and crashed to the floor. The creature was on top of him in an instant.

"Kill it now!" Abbott yelled. His eyes pleaded for salvation. Wesley raised his weapon, but failed to pull the trigger. "Please! You must—"

The monster pounced on its prey. Fangs bit through the man's neck; blood spurted from Abbott's exposed jugular. Abbott's fear did nothing to save him.

Neither did Wesley.

The agent fell back a step, one hand tight to his gun, and the other held out before the ravenous beast. Blood poured from the stained jaw of the monster, his pound of flesh clearly not enough—not with another target in reach.

"This doesn't need to go any further," Wesley said. He pointed to the portal. "You took my friend. I want him back."

The monster cocked its head at the agent. A question seemed to form on its lips, but the creature appeared unable to speak. Wesley pressed the issue.

"Joshua Falk," he said. "His name was Joshua Falk. Do you know what happened to him?"

The monster smiled knowingly.

Wesley's second hand took hold of his pistol. The pair shook in anger. "You recognized the name. Where is he? Tell me!"

The creature snarled. Claws swiped at the air, forcing Wesley back and away from the portal, which continued to crackle with energy. Lightning sparked from the well into the future, but did not spray out. It was being held in check—kept in reserve to buy time, but for what and for whom?

"He was a good man," Wesley said. "He was my friend. And I want him back."

The monster pounced. He wanted blood—Wesley's blood.

Wesley ducked under the strike. The monster slammed into the crates behind him. He rolled with the impact and was back on its feet before Wesley made it five steps away.

The portal remained open. Wesley could see the lightning streaking along the sides. It pulled in one direction and trailed after the movements of the beast in the room. The two were connected, locked in place together. One couldn't exist without the other.

Wesley didn't have any other options. The portal was his only link to Falk. It was the only way to save his friend. He couldn't let it fade away. He also couldn't allow his life to be forfeited because of its continued existence.

"Wes..." a voice called from the portal.

Wesley could see a figure inside—the shadow of a man. Darkness shrouded his face, except for the thick lenses that blocked his eyes from view. The outline of the figure showed off the man's fedora and trench coat as well.

"Falk," Wesley called. "Are you okay? Can you make it through the portal?"

Falk shook his head. "You have to shut it down, my friend."

"What?" Wesley asked. "I can't. I—"

"It's okay," Falk said through the portal. "This is what has to happen. Hurry before he—"

The monster launched at Wesley. The agent cried out as thick claws peeled away the flesh along his arm. Wesley stumbled back to the ground. Fangs snarled, ready to end his life.

Wesley looked at his friend. The shadow in the portal nodded acceptance at what was to come. Bitterness raged in the agent, but he held nothing back. Before the fangs of the monster penetrated his skin, Wesley raised his weapon to the primary controls of the console.

"I'm sorry I couldn't save you, my friend."

He opened fire. The shots shattered equipment and caused a spray of sparks to shower over the pair. The portal quaked at the loss of connection. It shimmered and faded. Around the outskirts of the glowing window into another time, streaks of purple light slipped loose.

They streaked wildly through the room. A bolt shot forward and stabbed the beast in the back. The monster bellowed with rage, not from the pain at the blow, but at the immediate effect the lightning had on him. Red eyes sparked and fangs gnashed the air as the monster was pulled back through the portal.

Wesley stared at the open doorway to the future. The shadow of his friend raised a single hand and waved. Then he was gone. So was the portal.

"Forgive me," Wesley whispered. Some might have argued that there had been no choice. Wesley knew better. The moment he'd failed to save Abbott, the second he'd brought Falk into the case in the first place, he had damned both men. He had stolen their futures as much as he had his own. Wesley sat in the warehouse's destruction with his hands over his swollen eyes. "Forgive me."

CHAPTER TWENTY-TWO

It took them an hour to maneuver through the late night traffic of the city. Jenkins' apartment was hidden behind a corner deli, the stairs tucked between twin dumpsters. The place smelled like rotten cheese and cigarette ash, not something Ben wished to come home to after a long day.

Four apartments occupied the second floor. Ben passed three of them. No lights were on; the occupants must have turned in earlier. Police tape marred the entry to the apartment in question. The tape crisscrossed the middle of the door, then wrapped around the handle to secure the room from evidence tampering.

Ben pulled out his keys and cut away the tape from the knob. It fell to his feet before he kicked it away. He reached to open the door, and Morgan's hand fell on his.

"Hold up a second," she whispered.

Ben tossed her a quizzical look, confused at the hesitation. She shifted in front of him. One hand held tight to her Glock, the other to a flashlight, which she clicked on to light their way. Ben's eyes rolled when she moved for the door.

"Morgan, I can—"

"Follow my lead," she said over him.

Ben grimaced, tired of playing the game with her. Her constant concern grated on his every nerve. The late hour, and lack of rest, didn't help his mood either.

"Go ahead," he said through gritted teeth.

She slipped into the darkness of the apartment. Her gun led the way. Ben didn't even try to follow. He remained in the hall, kicking at the police tape in frustration. Jenkins had died downtown, the search of his apartment merely a procedural move, not a critical component to the crime. Morgan, though, treated it like there was an actual threat to be found.

A threat wasn't even necessary at this point. Everything, in Morgan's opinion, was a danger for Ben. He might step on a rusty nail. There might be too much cholesterol in the burger he had for lunch. Everything was a concern for him, as if his life was hanging on by a thread in the aftermath of his near-death experience.

Morgan didn't see it that way, of course. She saw it as protection, not hampering him. He had let it slide since coming back to work, but it certainly annoyed the living shit out of him.

"Clear," Morgan called from the living room. She clicked on the light to guide Ben inside.

"Great." The place looked like the stockroom of a supply shop. Boxes lined the walls, tucked between furniture and under tables. Each was labeled, denoting the t-shirts, snow globes, and dozens of other contents contained within.

The rest of the apartment was drab. Most of the walls were bare, the paint faded from decades of neglect. The couches and tables were hand-me-downs, likely older than the victim. The entire place gave the impression of being a rest stop for the young man instead of an actual home.

Ben pointed to the bedroom, afraid to make a move without permission. "Can I do my job now?"

"What?" Morgan asked, not taking his meaning. "Something wrong?"

Only everything, he wanted to say, but held his tongue. "Nothing."

He stopped at the edge of the bedroom. His hand rested along the frame, and his fingers tightly squeezed the wood. Every instinct told him to focus on the work. There was a job to do, and he needed to fulfill it, but he couldn't hold it back any longer.

Ben spun to face his partner, who had begun searching the rest of the living room. "No, it isn't nothing."

"What's going on?"

"What the hell are we doing here, Morgan?"

Morgan blinked at the question, shocked at the anger behind his words. "Two men are dead."

"Which the police are handling," Ben said. He could feel the heat rising in his chest, and he fought to rein in his frustration. He focused every ounce through his hands as he leaned on the kitchen table chair before him. "We have more important things to do."

"More important things?" Morgan repeated. "Are you—"

"The Trust, Morgan!" Ben yelled. "They're out there, and we have no clue who they are or what they're after. We know nothing about the people who tried to wipe us out, and we won't if we don't focus on that."

"You think I don't want to?" Morgan moved for the door and closed it. They didn't need the rest of the floor listening to their argument. When she returned, Morgan shifted next to Ben. "You think I would be standing here if I had one clue, a single lead, on who those bastards are? That I wouldn't be hunting them down this very second if I knew anything that might help me bring them down?"

"We should be focusing on that," Ben seethed.

"This is what your problem has been this entire time? Why you pushed Wesley away instead of hearing him out?" Morgan shook her head. "That wasn't like you. That's not the Ben Riley who went to bat for Henry Reed in Chicago, determined to prove his innocence no matter what the evidence said."

"What good did it do?" Ben snapped. His hands flew from the chair, his arms flailing wildly in anger. "The kid is gone. Who knows what the hell they've done to him since we supposedly saved his life?"

"How many will die here today if we walk away?" Morgan answered. "Wesley deserves our help. Same as Henry did."

"At what cost?" Ben said with a sigh. He rubbed at his tired eyes, then fell back against the frame of the bedroom door.

"You should be resting." Morgan joined him along the wall.

"No," he said, shaking away the long day. "You're right. About Wes. I shouldn't have said those things to him. I should have believed him more."

"One way to make up for that." Morgan held out a hand to the room before them.

Morgan was right. Two people were dead, and if Wesley's information proved correct, there had to be some connection. They were targeted for a reason. The answer was in Jenkins' apartment, and Ben knew he had to find it. That was the only way to make things right.

"So do we have any idea who this Percival Jenkins was, or why our monster of the week made him a corpse?"

"That's my partner," Morgan said with a smile. She followed him into the bedroom. While he made a beeline for the closet for some insight into the man, Morgan headed for the desk. Picking at the receipts and open folders sitting atop the man's laptop, Morgan lifted one for Ben to see. "Looks like he owned a shop downtown. Bethesda Swag. Like people still say things like swag."

"They don't?"

Morgan ignored him, focusing on the inventory list on the paper. "He dealt in local memorabilia. T-shirts, postcards, and crap like that."

Ben chuckled. "So no 'I heart Bethesda' mug for you for your birthday?"

"I'm good," she said. She continued to dig through the paperwork on the desk. "As to why he was targeted by this thing? I have no clue."

Ben left the closet behind for the dresser in the far corner of the room. The drawers were neat and organized, something Ben could never aspire to be with his own setup. Glancing up at the photos lining the top, Ben paused on the one in front.

"I think I figured out the why," he said. She dropped the files and joined him at the dresser. He lifted the photo in question and passed it along to his partner.

It was an image of Jenkins at an award ceremony with the rest of his staff. They wore printed t-shirts denoting the local award for best business. Each shirt had the previous year stamped across them. Morgan noticed the connection immediately.

"This is Jenkins?"

Ben nodded. "Remind you of someone? The hair and the eyes?"

Morgan recalled a similar image from the DSA Archives. "He looks just like Wesley did fifty years ago."

"Exactly," Ben replied. He placed the image back where they found it. They started for the exit. They needed to get back to Wesley as quickly as possible. "You were right. His nightmare is real."

"Yeah," Morgan agreed. "And it's hunting him."

CHAPTER TWENTY-THREE

Wesley woke with a start. His chest heaved and sweat pooled along his temple. Sitting up, the old man shifted to the headboard to calm his nerves. He dabbed at the sweat over his brow, then ran his hands through thin strands of gray hair.

The nightmare stayed with him. Every moment was locked in place, never diminishing despite the decades between. Wes could still hear the rain pelting the sidewalk, and Falk's scream as he left this world.

The scream always remained. Wesley blamed himself. It was true that Falk was a grown man capable of making his own decisions, but Wesley had brought him into the fold. He had wanted a partner, someone to rely on for a case no one else had cared about. Falk had been the only one to join him.

The fool.

Tears stained Wesley's cheeks. He wiped them away, wishing the memory could just as easily be forgotten. Fifty years and still that night stuck with him. Falk shouldn't have been in that warehouse. The case had been Wesley's obsession, and it had caused a decent man to lose his life.

Wesley had taken that loss and tried to make it right. He committed the rest of his days to working with other like-minded agents around the country on cases buried and forgotten, or too downright bizarre to investigate. Over the years, they became more organized, and a name took root among them: the DSA. They dedicated themselves to the mysteries that plagued the world — those that hid in the shadows just out of view and could never truly be explained. The work, and his quest to save the life of the friend he had lost, caused Wesley to turn away from all thoughts of a normal life, of family and friends. His every effort went toward finding answers to questions undreamed of.

There had been good days because of that decision. Wesley had saved lives in his pursuits. He had never asked for recognition, never hoped for praise at the endless hours of investigation and the sleepless nights staking out the worst of the worst. His efforts had averted disasters, but only he knew about them in the end.

It was no wonder Ben and Morgan had failed to accept his story. He had hidden his work at the DSA. They had seen him as only an old man inserting himself into events that held no bearing on him, an old man past his prime and deserving of the hovel that the retirement home provided for him.

He was washed up and useless—broken down and angry at a life too long-lived.

Wesley left his bed in a huff. He shuffled to the window and the darkness outside. It was the only view he ever saw anymore, never the light of the sun and the hope of a brand-new day. Since Falk's disappearance, Wesley had been nothing but a shadow of a man.

He should never have pushed for action, should never have mentioned Falk or what happened so long ago. There was a man's death to consider first. That was where he should have started, and let Ben and Morgan take the next steps themselves. Instead, his fears had pushed the pair of DSA agents away. It was the same behavior he had employed with the men and women who surrounded him in his day-to-day activities.

"They were still wrong," Wesley muttered. His hand ran along the cold of the windowpane. The chill outside flowed through him. "They were still wrong to walk away. I need their help."

Howling screams filled the corridor of the home. Shadows ran under his door; hurried steps carried residents toward the exits. Wes pushed aside the guilt of the past as he shuffled quickly for the door.

Fear greeted him in the hall. People cried out, their words muttered and unclear. They were in too much of a hurry to escape, but escape from what?

Wesley knew it the moment the growl echoed from the lobby

of the retirement home. "Not now," he whispered.

Edna bumped into him and nearly toppled to the carpet. She held firm to his arm to steady herself. "Did you see it?" she cried.

Wesley shook his head.

Edna didn't bother waiting for more. She pushed from him and continued down the hall for the rear exit. Wesley, however, continued toward the lobby.

The monster turned the corner before Wesley had made it to his neighbor's door. All doubt left Wesley the moment the creature stepped into view. He knew the truth the second those red eyes caught sight of him.

The monster had come for him at last. The end had finally arrived for Wesley Fuller.

CHAPTER TWENTY-FOUR

They arrived within the hour. When the call came in, no questions were asked. An address and a target were whispered over the secure line, the voice on the other end obscured and masked to protect their anonymity. That was the work they had committed their lives to providing—helping those with the wherewithal to change the world, and the pocketbook to make it a reality.

The target was a man named Nixon Jessup.

Twin vans entered the property from the single lane access on the dirt road. It was a soft approach, subdued to avoid raising the target's suspicion on the property. Orders were given in hushed tones to the six paramilitary soldiers from their squad leader, communicated through headsets to those in the other van.

They dispersed the second they entered the clearing where the log cabin was positioned. Two to each side, they circled the property in a wide sweep. They remained low to the ground, the dim light from inside the property causing them to remain cautious in their movements. The intel passed along about the target was brief: the opposition appeared to be nothing more than a civilian with a fetish for the computer.

The squad leader knew better than to go in guns blazing, though. He had served three tours overseas and seen what recklessness in the field resulted in.

"Perimeter secured," his second-in-command said through the set. The two teams converged on the porch and took up positions around the front door.

"You are clear for insertion," the leader announced to the

team, his voice rattling in their ears.

The lock for the door fell away in less than a second. The door did not even creak under their entry—practiced and reassured from years of working together. All four raised their weapons—M16 assault rifles—and proceeded through the shallow hallway. The squad leader followed in reserve with his second-in-command.

"Clear in the kitchen," a voice called.

"Hall on the right is clear," another chimed through the headset.

"Eyes on the target?" the leader asked.

They rounded the small corridor that divided the broken up cabin until they came to the entrance of the main living space at the center of the domicile. A rerun of some sitcom from the 70s was on the television. The light from the screen cast a shadow against the wall next to their entry points.

The top of Nixon's head was visible from the top of the couch. He made no motion for them, completely unaware of their presence in the home.

The squad leader gave the go-ahead to his team, who approached from both sides of the target. Silencers kept the shots muted, but the damage was extensive. The top of the target's head exploded. Cushioning filled the air from the perforations along the back of the couch. The television screen shattered, and the room fell into complete darkness.

"Target down," the squad leader said. His voice boomed in the space. There was no need for subterfuge now. "I need cleanup in here."

His second nodded, then moved for the body. The moment he rounded the couch, he ripped the mask from his face. "Sir? It's not him."

"What?"

The squad leader joined his subordinate. He reached for the victim on the couch. The second his fingers touched what remained of Nixon's head, it fell to the floor and rolled for the corner. Straw and thick reams of paper were stuffed down the neck of the dummy body, which fell across the cushion. Anger consumed the squad leader. "Son of a bitch. A decoy?"

"He knew we were coming," one of the other men said. "We should—"

"Quiet," the squad leader snapped. This was still his operation, and he wouldn't have it fall apart immediately. He refused to allow his soldiers to lose their professionalism just because the job hit a snag. He turned to his second. "Find him. Search the rest of the damn place. Give me something we can use."

His team scattered, leaving him the room. He peered around. Nixon was a civilian, not a threat—not to someone who had seen as much violence and death as he had. Nixon might have been clever enough to vacate the premises, but not enough to do so without leaving behind something of value.

"What is this?" Shards of paper sprinkled the floor. They contained fragments of images and reports. On the wall leading to the stairs there appeared to be string connecting points, but the points had been removed—and recently, too.

His second returned. "Place is filthy. No clothes missing. He was here."

"Here's something," another voice said. The man pushed away the decoy body. There was a laptop sitting on the cushion.

"Why would he leave his computer here?"

The man shrugged. "It's on. I can—" He reached for the device, and lifted it from the couch. A small cord was attached. The line ran from the laptop through the cushion and underneath the piece of furniture.

The squad leader's eyes widened. "It's wired! Don't—"

The explosion shook the earth. It spread from the center of the log cabin in all directions. Secondary explosions erupted from the generator. Debris scattered throughout the clearing. It shattered the windows of the twin black vans parked out front, which caused their alarms to go off.

Kanigher watched the entire event unfold from the tree line east of the property. Flames filled the binoculars, the entire domicile consumed in an instant.

"That's one way to test a theory," he muttered.

Nixon sat against a nearby tree. He held tight to his tablet. His web of conspirators filled his laptop bag, the images and reports poking through the unclasped pocket.

"I'd ask where the explosives came from..."

Nixon smirked. "I wouldn't."

"I figured as much," Kanigher said. He shifted to his knees, then stood. "You all right?"

Nixon stared at the destruction with sadness in his eyes. "It belonged to my grandparents. They built it themselves. I always hated the place. Made me feel like I was hiding."

"Still," Kanigher said. "Not an easy thing to lose."

"No, I suppose not," Nixon replied. He moved to his feet, and the pair headed deeper into the tree line to get out of the light from the flames.

"About before…"

Nixon stopped. "I'm not some throwback, Agent. I'm not an anarchist, or some scalp hunter redskin."

"I never said you were," Kanigher said. "I said you were dangerous. This doesn't exactly disprove my thinking."

"It should," Nixon said. "You asked for sacrifice? This should show you how far I'm willing to go." He patted the side of his bag. "This matters to me."

Kanigher looked over the young man. He wanted to rail against him, to bring up the men and women who had died from his acts of terror on their lives. The stalwart agent always believed in the law. He sought to do the right thing for his country, yet what was right appeared to blur into deeper shades of gray than he'd thought possible. Suddenly, Nixon didn't appear to be the bad guy in the situation, or the danger Kanigher had once thought.

"Come on," Kanigher said. They cut through the woods until they reached the street. "We need to get to the exfil point before—"

The crack of twigs in the grass alerted Kanigher to their arrival. Kanigher pulled Nixon close, then reached for his weapon.

Four men stepped out of the shadows. They wore all black, their faces masked from view. They raised their weapons.

"Put it down," one demanded.

Kanigher held out for a long second to assess the threat level. A slight nod was followed by the lowering of his pistol. He kicked it away.

One man tapped the comm unit on his ear. "We have him, sir."

CHAPTER TWENTY-FIVE

The four men made no move against them. Kanigher continued to keep Nixon close, shielding him from their direct line of sight. It gave Nixon little in the way of comfort. All it took was one shot to put Kanigher down and then nothing would protect Nixon from their wrath.

The young man knew what was coming right from the start. Something in him had always known how his story would end. He'd spent years poking the bear. Eventually, only one response remained for him: an end he'd expected long before tonight.

Nixon was grateful Kanigher stood at his side. There was a time when he would never have considered working with others. His beliefs always ran counter to those around him—be it the kids at his foster home after losing his grandparents, or his peers in college. Nixon had always grated on everyone's nerves. He'd pushed their buttons so much, like a nervous compulsion, that loneliness was the only inevitable outcome.

Headlights cut through the darkness. A black sedan stopped short of their position on the road. The door opened, and a man wearing a shirt and tie entered the arena. He picked at his cufflinks, which sparkled against his shining white shirt.

"This is him?" the man asked.

"It is," one of the masked soldiers replied.

Nixon cursed. The insertion team was too obvious. Of course, a backup squad waited for them to leave the scene. He should have known better than to believe in a clean escape.

"You've caused me a lot of trouble this evening, young man," the gentleman said. "You've cost me a lot of money trying to put your so-called intel back in the bottle."

"I'm sorry."

"You should be," the man snapped.

Nixon shook his head. "No, I mean, I'm sorry, but I don't know who you are."

The man nearly stumbled. Laughter filled his cheeks, which shook as the sound erupted from his lips. "You don't know who I am? All you've done tonight and you don't even know who I am? I'm Bryant St. James, you little pissant."

Nixon jabbed Kanigher in the arm. "Told you."

Kanigher sighed. "You did."

"Wait, what?" the man asked.

"Did you get all that?" Kanigher said to the emptiness of the forest.

"Who?" the man's voice wailed into the night. His patience was clearly spent. "Who are you talking to?"

Nixon pulled out his tablet. It was on and recording. The screen showed the four men and St. James in the middle of the road—the vantage caused them to spin around in terror.

The shots came quickly. Each hit the mark. One by one, the masked soldiers fell. Their bodies littered the street, surrounding a stunned and terrified St. James.

Kanigher retrieved his sidearm. At the sight of the armed agent, St. James reeled. He stumbled back to his car and pried open the driver's-side door. A single shot shattered the window, and St. James stepped out of the vehicle with his hands up.

"What do you people want from me?"

"From you?" a voice called from the tree line. Metcalf climbed down from her perch. The sniper rifle hung tight to her back as she entered the street. "Not a damn thing, Bryant."

"Then what was this all about?"

"This is a message to your friends in the Trust," Metcalf said.

"You're insane," St. James said. "You have no idea what you're up against."

"But we will," she replied. There was no emotion in her voice, not even the slightest bit of anger. It startled Nixon, the lack of anything in Susan Metcalf. His own anger was impossibly difficult to contain. What the Trust had done to the world needed to be known by all. To Metcalf, it was only the next mission.

"Then tell me," St. James said. "Tell me your all-important

message to pass along to this so-called Trust."

Metcalf ran her tongue along her teeth. His words stung her: his refusal to admit the Trust's existence, just like all the rest. She raised her sidearm at the man.

"Here's my message."

The shot caught him in the chest. St. James stood for a split-second, a look of shock spread across his face, then collapsed against the side of his car. His body slumped over in a heap along the pavement.

"W-W-What?" Nixon asked, trying to find the words. He stared at the fallen figure. "You… you killed him?"

"Nixon…" Kanigher moved between them.

Nixon shook his head, pushing through the agent for the side of the car. "Why did you kill him?"

"Nixon," Metcalf said in a calm voice. She bent over St. James and rolled him to his side. His chest rose and fell in a slow rhythm. "It was a tranquilizer."

"You mean he's not…" Nixon struggled to catch his breath.

"None of them are," Kanigher said. The four armed guards lay unconscious around them, sleeping through a massive dose of whatever Metcalf had shot them with.

"Why not?" Nixon asked, suddenly aware of their continued presence at the scene, and the threat they had posed to his life mere seconds ago.

"Wait…" Metcalf said. "Are you mad we did kill them, or that we didn't kill them?"

"Sounds like both to me," Kanigher chimed in.

"I wish I knew," Nixon admitted. He ran his hands over his face.

Kanigher grinned. "We need them alive."

Metcalf nodded. "St. James is a single link in a larger chain. We need to see where he can lead us. Have anything that might help us with that?"

Nixon slowly caught her eyes as they fell upon his bag. He dropped the contents to the ground and dug through until he found what she needed. Meanwhile, Kanigher collected the phones of those lying around the scene. He brought them over, careful to lay each in the corresponding direction of their owner.

Working rapidly, Nixon removed the back of each phone to replace them with a bug of his own personal design. As he finished with each, Kanigher returned them. During the exchange, Metcalf slipped inside the cab of the sedan. She tucked a device under the dash, and another beneath the seat. They were listening devices and physical trackers, all set to monitor St. James closely.

With the task complete, Metcalf helped Nixon collect his gear. He strapped the bag to his shoulder once more and stood to face the pair. "I'm not used to having to thank people. Especially for saving my ass multiple times in a single day. I don't usually find myself in quite so many jams…"

"Yeah, we have that effect on people," Kanigher said, though his attention focused on Metcalf when he said it.

Nixon's brow furrowed. He started to ask what the agent meant, but Metcalf stepped in.

"We should move. They won't be out much longer, and we need to put some distance between us."

Kanigher and Metcalf started down the road for their waiting car. Nixon stayed behind, half locked on the burning structure that had served as his home and half on the sleeping crew sent to kill him.

"Susan…" he called.

Metcalf stopped. "They planned to kill you, Nixon, just for knowing the truth." Her eyes were cold daggers of blue against the stark black of night. "This is what we're fighting against, Nixon. I'm sorry we dragged you into it like this."

"I…"

Metcalf's hand fell on his shoulder. "I want you with us. I want your help to bring these bastards down. Every single one of them. But you have to know what that means. All of it."

Nixon stared at the threat he had unlocked through his deeds. In his arrogance to prove his point to Kanigher, Nixon had brought them right to his doorstep and thrown away his life in the process. There was no more safety here, nor did he think he would ever find it again.

"I understand," Nixon said.

"You can walk away, Nixon," Metcalf said.

He knew the truth, however. Between the cops earlier and the loss of his grandparent's home tonight, there was no walking away for him. This was the fight he had been preparing for, and these were the soldiers that were going to help him succeed.

"I'm in, Susan," he said. "All the way."

Metcalf nodded. "Looks like we have our work ahead of us. Don't you agree, Agent Kanigher?"

Kanigher sneered at the woman. He had fought against welcoming Nixon for most of the day, but could no longer do that. He patted Nixon on the back.

"Welcome to the DSA."

CHAPTER TWENTY-SIX

Someone was screaming.

Zac woke to a blur. A chaos of light swirled through his startled vision. Everything spun around him like a carousel. From stark black to an array of colors, Zac struggled to find his way back to consciousness.

"What happened here?" Nancy yelled. What was she doing in his room? "My God, what have you done?"

"Huh?" Zac struggled to move, unable to stand because of a colossal weight on his legs. Cables stretched over him, pinning him to the floor in the center of the room. His voice echoed from the vaulted ceiling. "Where am I?"

Zac shook the colors away. He had been lost to a dream, yet remembered nothing from the events of his slumber. They had been fragmented images, so much like the world around him now, that it frightened him.

Nancy stood at a distance. She wore a purple bathrobe, and she clutched it tighter when his eyes fell on her. Her beaming smile no longer greeted him, only pure terror at being in his presence. Micah laughed from beside her. He snapped images with his phone in rapid succession.

His laughter echoed in Zac's ears. "The spaz has finally lost it."

"Nancy? Micah?" Zac asked. "What am I doing here? This isn't the guest room."

"No shit, jackass," Micah replied.

Nancy slapped his arm, but said nothing about his language. Her hand rested along her son's arm, pulling him away from their guest. There was no more warmth and compassion in her, only a fear that saddened Zac.

The room fell into focus. He was in the living room, though it was a pale reflection of the space he had spent so little time in over the last three weeks. The couch was overturned, with cushions removed and their stuffing laid in clumps all over the room.

Nancy's personal computer sat gutted on the floor. Every circuit board and wire was pulled loose from the tower. The wires were strung together in thick groups, connected to more wires from the television, the DVD player, and more. All kept Zac strapped to the floor, yet was not the end of the nightmare.

Writing covered the walls — painted there from the open and spilled supplies in the room's corner. Words and equations, fragments of thoughts, were scattered in disarray. Paint covered every image hanging on the walls, the musings of the painter not confined to open wall space.

Hands covered in the earthy tan color made it clear to Zac who the painter truly was. "What happened?"

"Oh, wow," Micah said, unable to rein in his laughter. "This is like full mental patient stuff. Way to pick 'em, Ma."

"Knock it off, Micah," Nancy said. It wasn't in the motherly tone she had shown at dinner. The rebuke was muted, her voice little more than a whisper. "Zac?"

"I don't remember coming down here," Zac said. His gaze flitted about the room. Each pause snapped another image of the writing on the walls. Math was involved, quantum relations the likes of which he had never seen before. Zac shifted the cables from his legs and fought for his feet. At the movement, Nancy jumped back. "I'm not going to hurt you. I would never — "

"This was my living room," Nancy snapped. "Look what you did to my home!"

"I didn't..." Zac stopped. There were locations, geo-coordinates listed. He tried to figure them out, but the staggering shuffle of Nancy's slippers pulled him back. "I wouldn't have done this. Whatever this is."

The fear melted from Nancy. She took a step forward, fire in her eyes. "How? How can you look at it — at me — and think for a second that I would believe you didn't put it there?"

Micah lifted the phone. "We caught the end of your crazy before you collapsed in the middle of the room. Jackass."

The recording started for Zac and made everything clear.

Fingers danced along the walls. The mutterings of a madman slipped from his lips as he worked. Cables sparked, lights blew out behind him, but they did nothing to deter him from the task.

"I did this," Zac said when the video ended.

"All of this!" Nancy shouted. "Every last lunatic phrase. You destroyed my home! I opened my door to you and you ruined my home!"

"Nancy, I..."

She shook her head, refusing to listen to a single word of it. "I want you out. Right now. This very instant!"

"I can fix this, Nancy," Zac said. He couldn't, of course. He didn't have a clue how he had done it. The wire connections, the snaking cables around the room that twisted into sockets in different appliances, made no sense—like he was trying to tap into something.

Whatever the message meant, however, remained out of reach. The walls became a secondary method to work through the problem, as he might have done at the DSA, sketching out thoughts on the whiteboards of the briefing room or in a notebook during breaks.

"You have to let me try."

"No, I don't," Nancy said. She reached for the phone in its cradle. "I will call the police in ten minutes if you aren't out of here."

"That phone... probably doesn't work," Zac said with a cringe.

Nancy threw the device to the ground. "Ten minutes, Micah. Then call the police."

"Gladly, Ma," Micah said with a shit-eating grin.

Nancy started for the stairs. She was done with him, just like Claire and everyone else in his life. "Nancy, whatever this is... I would never try to... I mean, I don't even know what this is. What it means. I need to figure it out, need to see why I would do something like this. Let me—"

The bedroom door slammed shut, ending his pleading.

Zac rubbed at his swollen eyes. "Crap."

The light of a flash caused him to turn. Micah continued to snap images on his phone. "Nine minutes, jackass. You better be gone."

Zac watched the kid depart from the room to check on his

mother.

"What have I done?" Zac asked in the silence of the room. He kicked the cables at his feet away, nearly stumbling to escape their snare. The walls continued to call to him, but he had to pack. Two phrases repeated throughout the living space in thick, bold letters, as if they were more important than the rest.

THE SIGNAL
TERMINAL POINT

Zac's fingers brushed against the dried paint on the wall, almost willing it for an answer. "Better still, what the hell does it all mean?"

CHAPTER TWENTY-SEVEN

"Everyone, run!"

Chaos consumed the corridor. Wesley had thought himself alone with the menace from his past. For a brief second, they were the only two beings in the world, staring each other down as if caught in a high noon showdown. When the world returned to focus, the crowds of the retirement village filled Wesley's view.

Screams rang out. They were cries of panic and pain. No one understood what was happening. No one saw the threat for what it was.

Ernie tried. Dumb and intolerant Ernie, who never cared for the job, let alone the people in the place, was the only one to confront the beast in their midst. His fist flew faster than his mouth, the curse words mitigated by shock as the man-monster caught the blow with ease. The monster tossed Ernie to the side, and the attendant crashed into the drywall.

Wesley wanted to help. He fought to get his body in motion to intervene. Nothing worked. Fear held him tight, the same terror that had stolen his life away like he had been shunted into the time portal instead of Joshua Falk.

Ernie scrambled from the hole his body had created in the wall. The creature leaped on top of him before he stood. Jaws snapped wide; the monster's teeth were sharp as fangs and double set like a shark's. Ernie's panicked eyes pleaded for Wesley — for anyone — to save him.

No one did.

Blood dripping from his lips, the monster dropped his victim to the carpet. Crimson stained the periwinkle blue, and spread from the dead man, whose eyes continued to burrow into Wesley.

The screams of the others in the hall intensified. Those who hoped for intervention woke to the reality of their situation and rushed to escape the building. For some, however, it was too late. The monster cut through them like a scythe through crops. Bodies flew in all directions, and crumbled against furniture and through open doorways.

"Hey," a voice called from behind Wesley. "Wesley?"

Wesley nearly jumped when a hand fell on his shoulder. He spun to see Edna at his side.

"What?" Wesley muttered, his voice so dry from staring at the torturous pain of those around him. "What are you doing here? Why did you come back?"

Edna ignored him. "We need to leave."

"I... I can't."

"He's not human," she said. "Those teeth? Those eyes? He's what you saw that night. What you were trying to tell us?"

Wesley nodded. He didn't think she had been listening, that she'd cared to know anything about him after all their fighting and bickering.

"It's my fault."

"Nothing that thing does is your fault, Wesley," Edna replied. "Now come on."

"No," Wesley said. He pulled away from her sharply. It wasn't what he intended, and he drew her hand to his chest with a soft touch. "You're right. You are. I'm not talking about what he's done. I'm talking about what I've done. Or what I haven't done."

"What do you mean?"

"I can't keep running, Etta," Wesley said. "I have to face him. Here and now, or this will never end. Not for me."

"Wesley..."

"Go," he said, letting her loose. "Help the others."

"What are you going to do?"

It was a good question, and one that deserved an answer—for his own comfort, at the very least. Instead, Wesley gave the only response he could. "Whatever I can."

She offered a slight nod, then started for the rear exit. At the door to the common room, she turned back toward him. "And it's Edna, you senile old fool."

A smirk grew on his face. "I know."

He waited for her to make it through the door. He watched her help a man who had been hiding in the corner to his feet. After the pair was out of sight, Wesley turned to face the beast once more.

The monster ripped through furniture. He gnashed his teeth in the air, snapping at tables and chairs. Claws slashed at the ground. Nothing would stand in his path, especially not an old man who had lived his entire life in fear because of what he'd seen that horrible night so long ago.

"No," Wesley whispered. It was time to push past that line of thinking. It was time to stop running and start doing what he should have done the night he lost his partner.

Wesley left the hallway behind. He tuned out the cries for help and the screams, and entered his room in a hurry. At his bed, he dropped to his knees. His hands dug through the boxes of memories—the few treasured possessions he'd kept all those years—until he found what he was looking for.

The box was heavy in his hands. He flipped off the lid. Inside, he saw the revolver, dingy from neglect. He wondered if the damn thing would work at all, but it was a risk Wesley had to take. His personal demon stood before him, and it was time to stand up and face it.

Bullets rattled along the bottom of the box. He reached inside to snatch what he could. Some slipped from his grasp to the ground. Wesley shoved those that remained into the revolver before closing the chamber.

He lifted the small weapon before him. "This will be enough. It has to be."

Wesley turned for the door, and the beast stood in the frame. The monster salivated at the sight of Wesley, anticipation in his dead eyes.

Wesley leveled the revolver at the monster that had haunted his days for decades. "Please, God. Let this be enough."

CHAPTER TWENTY-EIGHT

Morgan and Ben were barely in the parking lot when the doors opened. Bursting from within came a swath of people, both residents and employees, out into the chilly night. Screams rose as they rushed to escape. There was no pattern to their movements, no thought other than the need to save themselves.

"Well, that can't be good," Ben said. "Unless you think they're really excited about the Blizzard of the Month at Dairy Queen?"

"It's mint," Morgan replied. "Ain't no one excited about that."

Ben forced a laugh, clearly trying to fill the void of their silence since leaving Jenkins' apartment. Inside, he was hurting more than he let on, but while Morgan had focused on the physical aspects, she'd failed to consider the psychological. He wanted to hurt someone for what happened to him. He wanted to get the people hiding in the shadows.

Morgan tried to keep him focused on the one no longer hiding at all. Tires squealed to a halt next to the sidewalk, and Morgan threw the vehicle into park. Both hopped out of the car. Bystanders parted in their presence, like ripples in the ocean, and they were the boulder at the center.

Blood covered the walls inside the retirement home. Morgan noticed the bodies tucked behind the reception desk, both of the supervising attendants they had met earlier, and the security guard on duty.

She pulled out her sidearm. "Stay here in case it comes outside."

She took a step forward, formulating a plan of attack. The

home was immense, with too much room to cover on her own. Still, it was a safer bet to keep Ben in reserve, just in case the situation was worse than they knew.

Ben, however, offered her an answer she hadn't expected. "No."

"What?" she asked. He moved beside her, gun in hand and ready to head into danger. "Ben, I need you to —"

"Stay out of the line of fire, out of any kind of danger?" Ben shot back. He blocked her from the building. "Yeah, I got that. If it was up to you, I'd be in the Bunker, playing pinochle with Adler while you handle everything."

"I don't have time for this," Morgan snapped. She pushed through him. His hand caught her by the arm and held tight.

"Make the time."

"I'm just…"

"Just what?"

Morgan huffed. "You were shot, Ben. I'm trying to —"

"Don't you dare say protecting me," Ben said. "I am not some civilian, and I am through talking about what happened to me."

"Ben…"

"I'm not done." Ben let her go, backing up for the front doors to the complex. "Now I admit I'm not the happy-go-lucky guy I've been in the past. I'm angry about what happened. Furious, in fact. I was wrong to take it out on Wesley. Wrong to dismiss this case because of my own personal issues."

"Glad to hear you say that."

"But," he continued, and a sigh of aggravation escaped her. "You have to stop holding me back. I am your partner in this, Morgan. It's time to trust in that again. I can't make that call for you. It has to be yours."

He was right, of course. She had done her best to ignore his frustration over the last few weeks. Whenever she'd questioned his health, there was a palpable tension, one she had created by pushing the issue. She couldn't help it. Part of her would always look at those around her as a doctor would a patient instead of as a friend or a colleague — and even a partner.

Ben had taken it all in stride. Sure, there had been a comment or two to warn her of his anger, but mostly Ben had played along. He had given her time to accept the past and move on. That time was up.

Morgan looked at her partner and nodded. "Ben, when I found you in that classroom… when your heart stopped and your eyes closed? I've never been so scared in my life. I can't go through that again."

"I made a choice," Ben said.

"A stupid and reckless one," Morgan shot back.

"I'm full of them, Morgan," Ben said. "That's how I'm wired. That's the job, and I need you to let me do it again without the overprotective mother routine."

Seeing him like that, dying without a chance of surviving, still brought her to tears. The image ate away at her common sense until only the cold calculation of Morgan Dunleavy remained. It was the same coldness that had saved her brother's life at the expense of three others: the same one protecting her feelings and her heart from pain and loss.

"Ben, I…"

Ben grabbed the handle of the door, ready for what lay ahead without regard to his own safety. He only ever thought about others, the way Morgan always wanted to be.

"Come on, Morgan," Ben said. He cocked his head to the blood on the walls within. "Be stupid with me."

She stood in silence for a second, hearing his grand argument concluded with the absolute cheesiest thing she'd ever heard. Morgan shook her head. "I hate you."

"Your lips say hate, but your heart says love."

"Keep it up and I will shoot you."

Ben chuckled as the pair rushed through the reception area. "That's the Morgan I know."

They turned toward the residence wing on the first level. More destruction awaited them. The walls appeared shredded, and furniture had been upended. Civilians cried out in pain, cuts and gashes along their skin from their attacker. Ben and Morgan pushed harder to reach their target.

From the end of the corridor, a single shot rang out. It shattered the silence of the complex and took with it every last ounce of hope that they were not too late.

CHAPTER TWENTY-NINE

The shot woke them to the situation. Ben ran deeper into the retirement home. He had to set the record straight with Morgan, so she would see him as an equal member of their partnership again, but the conversation took precious time.

It was time Wesley didn't have.

The second shot battered back the killer. He staggered into the hallway, clearing the doorway for Wesley to escape. The old man rounded the corner, a look of surprise on his face at the sight of the two DSA agents heading for him.

"Wesley!" Ben cried out. "Come on, we need to get you out of here."

"Um, Ben?" Morgan said at his side. She pointed past the fleeing figure of Wesley Fuller.

The killer was still on his feet. It was clear Wesley's shots connected. The two holes in the man's chest attested to that. Their effect, however, had been minimal. Blood poured from the wounds, then slowed almost as if by will. The thin streams darkened; the crimson shifted to black, before both stopped completely.

Ben raised his weapon to greet the killer. "Wesley, get down!"

He opened fire. The killer ducked behind Wesley for cover to avoid the shots, which connected with the wall at the far end of the corridor.

Wesley tried to duck, his legs unable to comply with the simple command. Instead, his feet tripped on the thick carpet, and he tumbled forward. Claws ripped the air as he fell. Missing merely frustrated the monster even more.

"Ben, what are you doing?" Morgan asked. She tried to take out the threat, but Ben jumped in front of her.

There wasn't time for another shot. The bullets had done little to impede the beast from his intended target. The only avenue left was the physical.

"Something stupid, Morgan," Ben yelled as he ran at the monster. "What else?"

Wesley hugged the ground. The shadow of the killer loomed over him. He closed his eyes, a last prayer on his lips.

Ben leaped over Wesley into the beast. He slammed into the killer's midsection and sent them both crashing to the carpet. Ben rolled off. He shook off the effects of the collision as he made his way back to his feet. The killer was already running toward him, red eyes beaming through the darkness of the hall.

"Ben!"

Ben waved Morgan off as the beast swiped at him. The attack forced him back toward the common area. Claws sliced through drywall and the wood molding around the entryway like five knives through soft cheese.

"Get Wesley out of here, Morgan," Ben said.

The monster heard this and turned back to his target. Morgan helped Wesley to his feet. They were moving too slowly. Ben clenched his fist tight and let loose on the beast. The monster met his punch straight on. His head slammed to the right from the blow, but he remained on his feet.

Pain shot up Ben's arm. His whole body screamed from the impact. It was like hitting a concrete wall instead of flesh, like the man had a metal skeleton instead of bone.

"I said, go!" Ben shouted. He punched at the beast again. This time, the killer caught the blow and twisted his arm. Ben stumbled back, trying to pull his arm away without success. The pressure was incredible and he could feel the strain. It wouldn't take much more force to break Ben's arm.

Shots rang out. The killer bellowed as the bullets perforated his back. Ben was forgotten for a moment. His arm screamed with relief as Ben tucked the wounded limb close. He fell back a step, out of the line of fire.

Morgan emptied her clip into the monster. Every shot was center mass. She left nothing to chance. All, however, had been absolutely pointless. Her shock at seeing the truth was clear. "It can't be," she muttered, though the words echoed in the emptiness of the home. "It's just like—"

The beast pounced at her. The jump carried him into the hall, and right in front of the startled Morgan. Its arm swung wide, and the back of its hand crashed into Morgan's side. She soared away from the creature. Her battered body landed against the wall and slid to the ground.

"Morgan!"

Ben shuffled at the beast. His arm was nearly useless. Still, he needed to act. He needed to save his partner and Wesley, who continued to stand in abject terror in the center of the corridor.

His left hand flew out. The monster barely noticed the glancing strike. Slowly, the monster turned to face him once more. There was no anger on his face, only annoyance at yet another delay. He grabbed Ben by the wrist and flipped him over its shoulder. Ben collided with the struggling Morgan, and the pair crumpled in a heap.

"This really isn't going our way," Ben said, wincing in pain.

Morgan pushed him off. "I've seen this before, Ben. This is like Grissom. What the Trust did to him. We need—"

"No," Wesley called from the far end of the hall. "Not we. I have to do this."

"Wes, you can't. He's—"

Morgan raised her hand to cut him off. "Head shot, Agent Fuller. Make it count."

Wesley raised the revolver and took aim. The killer flashed its fangs at the shaking hands of the old man.

"You don't get to own my life anymore," Wesley said. "I won't let you."

The beast jumped at Wesley. When the gun went off, it forced Wesley back a step at the recoil. The bullet connected between the red eyes of the killer, who fell from the impact. The red of his eyes melted away to reveal twin pupils, and the man underneath the shell of a monster.

"Wesley!" Ben fought for his feet before rushing to the side of the exhausted senior. "Are you all right?"

The old man reached for a nearby chair for support. The revolver shook in his hand until he let it slip free. It clattered to the ground. "I... I think so."

Ben looked back at his partner. She crouched close to the deceased killer, sadness in her eyes. "Morgan?"

"It's a uniform," Morgan said. "I didn't notice it before, but he's… he's wearing a uniform. Like a soldier."

"That doesn't mean it's the same as Grissom."

Morgan shook her head. "He is." She ran her hand along the dead man's arm. "He's definitely better designed than Grissom, but the same work was done to him. The circuitry beneath the surface, controlled and refined into the perfect killing machine."

"Not that perfect," Ben replied. He cocked his head over to Wesley. Morgan nodded and let the dead go. It was time to care for the living.

"He was after me for so long," Wesley said. He clasped his shaking hands before him. "I never thought, never believed, I would be rid of him." He stared at the dead. "Now I see him for what he is: just a man. This whole time, my whole life, he's been the monster in my nightmares, haunting me for decades. But he's just a man."

Morgan removed her flashlight from her pocket. The beam was bright in the hallway's darkness. She shined it at Wesley's eyes. "I want to look you over, Wesley. Make sure you're—"

"I'm fine, Agent," Wesley said. He lowered the light from his eyes. Small tears dripped down his cheeks. "I'm better than fine."

He glanced up at Ben with a smile on his face, the first genuine joy they had seen from the man since meeting him.

"It's finally over."

CHAPTER THIRTY

"Now boarding at Platform Seven. All passengers for Washington, DC, boarding has started at Platform Seven."

People scurried in all directions. Even given the predawn hour, a crowd filtered through the terminal. Parents prodded their children forward, suitcases in tow. Workers prepared for their daily travel, newspapers and laptops at their sides. Murmurs muted the announcements, but Zac heard the reminder as he waited for his change at the ticket counter.

The woman plopped down the last of his dishwasher earnings. His ticket sat on top. "There you go."

"Thank you," Zac replied. Dry paint still covered his hands, and the woman offered him a curious glare. A disarming chuckle escaped his lips. "Rough night."

"I'll bet," the woman answered. She pointed to the highlighted sign at the end of the terminal. "Platform Seven is on the far end. It will take a few minutes to load, but you might want to hurry."

Zac shuffled his change into his pocket. He kept the ticket secure against his palm for fear of losing it. His duffel bag felt like a giant weight against his back, but he kept it in place as he moved out of line for the waiting platform.

Shaking away his exhaustion while he fought through the milling patrons of the bus terminal, excitement filled Zac at the prospect of seeing his wife. Bethesda was only a few hours away. So was his chance to correct the mistakes of his past... and the opportunity to figure out what was wrong with him.

The images continued to haunt him, the words on the walls and the cables knotted around his being. What the hell had he been doing? How could he have lost control of himself so completely?

None of it made sense. Claire would help with that. Of course she would. No matter the strife, the failures of the last few months, love would win out.

It had to for Zac.

Without Claire, without a chance at reconciliation, he had nothing else. There was no work to turn to, and no friends remained to support him. Every bridge had been burned to ash. Claire was his last lifeline.

The ticket agent waited impatiently at Platform Seven. "Sir? We're boarding, sir."

"I know," Zac said, the ticket still in his hand. "I—"

His stomach lurched. A cramp caused him to cry out, and he nearly stumbled into the woman at the gate.

"Hey!"

Zac tried to find his balance. His guts screamed for attention, his bladder suddenly full. "I have to go."

"Sir?"

Zac spun around for the restroom across the corridor. "I need a minute. Please!"

He pushed through people, his duffel bag swinging against everyone unfortunate to be passing by at the moment. He uttered apologies, but they were lost behind the hand covering his lips—afraid of what might come out after the words were spoken. His entire body revolted against him. It demanded attention rather than waiting for the bus to get under way.

A man tried to exit the bathroom at the exact second of Zac's arrival. "Watch it, jackass!"

Zac blinked hard to see if Micah had somehow followed him to the terminal. Instead, he was confronted by a middle-aged man in coveralls who cradled an unlit cigarette between his fingers.

"Sorry," Zac said. He shifted aside to give the man room. "I'm sorry. Excuse me."

Zac dropped his duffel just inside the door and raced for the first open stall. The door fought against him, but he kept it open with a hand as he dropped to his knees. They slammed against the tile. His head sank into the bowl.

Everything inside him left in a violent rush. Where it all came from because of his reduced appetite astounded him, yet with each heave, more found its way free from his guts.

He wasn't sure how much time passed during the event. It wasn't until the door swung open and the woman from the gate looked in that he realized he was still on his hands and knees.

"I'm sorry, sir," she said. "The bus left."

Zac didn't bother to look at her. "Okay."

"Should I call someone for you? A doctor, maybe?"

Zac shook his head. "No. I... I'll be fine. Thank you."

"Right," the woman whispered. Another gentleman passed her. She took it as her cue to depart. The man noted Zac's presence on the floor, and the foul stench from the stall, before joining her.

Content with everything out of his system, and that he had a modicum of privacy thanks to his sudden illness, Zac pushed away from the rancid toilet. His legs were shaky, but kept him standing as he moved for the sink. He filled his hands with water and splashed his face to wipe away the dregs running from his lips.

"What's wrong with me?" Zac asked. He watched the water swirl around the sink, then reached for the paper towels next to the counter. He pried them loose to dab his face. "What is happening to me?"

Zac tossed out the towels. He settled along the edge of the sink and let out a long breath. When he brought his gaze back up to the man in the mirror, his own reflection was no longer present. In its place was another face.

"What the hell?"

The voice he had been hearing became clear to him. There had been no other presence when he'd heard it at the Vroman home or at the diner. He had been alone. Or, at least, he thought he had been alone.

The voice had been inside him all along, and came from a dead woman Zac never thought he would see again.

April Newton stared back at him. The woman known as the Wellspring offered a satisfied smirk. "I think we should probably have a chat, don't you?"

CHAPTER THIRTY-ONE

Police surveyed the scene at the retirement home. They set to cleaning up the area immediately upon arriving. Combes took the lead, barking orders at every member of her team—sometimes with three or four follow-up instructions to keep them moving.

Ben did his best to stay out of her way, grateful when Wesley retired to his room in the aftermath. The officers cordoned off the corridor from residents but opened up the common rooms to filter in their return. Residents hung close together; they helped each other as much as the rest of the staff. Doctors raced between patients to ensure that everyone was seen and heard, and to get their lives back on stable ground quickly.

Ben wondered if such a thing was possible. That question, more than any other, carried over to their primary subject of concern. Wesley stared out his window, the darkness of the night dropping his eyes into shadow.

Morgan stepped inside, her reflection caught in the window. Wesley turned at her approach. "How is everyone?"

"Coping." Morgan took a seat on the edge of the bed. "They've brought in some outside help to see to any health issues. There will be some lingering nightmares, and a resident or two who will never believe a man went on a rampage through here, but eventually the rumors will subside and life will go on."

"Rumors," Wesley said with a chuckle. "You mean the truth."

They all smiled at his remark. Ben had seen it firsthand since coming aboard the DSA: the inability of the public to see the world for the way it was. There was always going to be some reticence to thinking outside the box, to believe in the nightmares that could exist without them stabbing you in the damn face.

Combes asked for the truth. All Ben and Morgan could give her was a story about a man out for revenge against Wesley. When pressed for a reason, mental illness had been offered. An excuse, though how far off remained unknown. Why he would have targeted Wesley above all else still made no sense.

Ben doubted it ever would. His hand fell on Wesley's shoulder. "I should have believed you from the start, Wesley. I'm sorry about that. Truly."

Wesley smirked. "Who would believe a cranky old man?"

Ben shook his head. "You mean a DSA agent."

"Always." Morgan stood to join them.

Wesley swiped at his eyes. "Thank you. Both of you."

The trio moved for the door. Forensics handled the dead, tarps covering both killer and victims alike. It would be a long time before life returned to normal in the retirement village, but Wesley wasn't the one to earn that concern. He seemed stronger since the end, and more confident to handle whatever life threw at him. There was none of the frustration or bitterness from before.

"I never asked, Wesley, but did you recognize him?" Morgan asked. "Was he the man from the warehouse that night?"

"He was," Wesley answered. "A spitting image of my nightmare."

"Who was he, though?" Ben's question resonated with each of them. "His shirt—uniform, if Morgan is right—read Tracker-282. Any idea what that means?"

"All good questions," Wesley replied. "But I'm not the one to know such things."

"Are you—"

Morgan held Ben up when Wesley stepped deeper into his room. Her eyes caught his, and the pair read each other instantly. Plenty of questions had been answered. Others would have to wait until later, and out of the presence of a tired former agent.

"Right," Ben whispered.

"We should check in with Combes," Morgan said. "See if she needs anything."

"Good point. We should—"

"Agent Riley," Wesley interrupted. "Could I borrow you for a moment before you leave?"

Morgan pushed Ben ahead, a quiet nod passing between them. She headed for Combes in the common room, a chore Ben was more than willing to avoid considering his previous interaction with the woman. Of course, that was how most of his conversations went with people these days. It was all sarcasm and deflection, rather than any level of connection. Looking back at Wesley, Ben wondered if he was on the same path as the elderly agent—and how the hell he could course-correct before it was too late.

"What's going on?"

"I wanted you to have something." Wesley moved for his bed and kneeled to retrieve the belongings tucked beneath. He returned his revolver to the box, then set to work digging through the rest of the junk that had accumulated. Files piled at his side. They were all worn from age, their covers faded and the lettering on each marred by time's unkind passage. "After what happened that night with Falk, I buried myself in my work. I did everything I could to find him, yet not enough to escape the monster from my nightmares. After a decade, however, I couldn't any longer. I..."

Wesley paused for a second. He clung tight to a photo in his hands.

"What is it?"

"Something I dropped earlier," Wesley said. He pointed to the empty frame on the shelf. "An old photo from better days." He tucked it in the middle of the files, hesitated for a brief second, and then let it rest where he'd put it.

"Wes, you don't have to—"

"These are for you." Wesley lifted the pile up to the bed. They crashed on the mattress and spread out before Ben.

"Old casefiles?" Ben reached for the closest one. The dates all read from the 1970s. "You've kept them all these years?"

Morgan had mentioned how there had been little to nothing from Wesley in the DSA's archives. It was as if they had been omitted, she'd believed. The truth, however, had been that much simpler: Wesley had hidden them away instead.

"Systems have a way of being compromised," Wesley said, joining his work on the bed. "The DSA was started by people, and it should have stayed that way. I knew that right from the start."

"You don't have to give these to me," Ben said. "This is your work."

"And now it's yours."

"Wes," Ben started in a soft voice. "I don't deserve... I mean, after what I said to you?"

"That's why these are for you," Wesley said. "You might have faltered at the start, but you were there at the end. You saw this through, just like you'll see these through."

"What do you mean?" Ben pawed through the top files. Names and dates blurred before him. There were no connections to be seen, no details to be gleaned from what he noticed at first glance. "What do these have to do with—"

"The Trust," Wesley said. The name stopped Ben cold. "These will help in your search."

"How did you know about them? How could you—"

"This is the fight ahead of you, Agent Riley," Wesley said. "You're going to need all the help you can get. Even from the unlikeliest of sources."

Ben took the files, and his hand ran along the surface. They felt heavy, like the contents within had weighed down Wesley's life for the last five decades, and the burden now passed to Ben.

"Is that a gut feeling?"

"The truth," Wesley said. "Never stop searching, Ben. Never stop questioning. It's only in the questions that mysteries are solved. No matter how much we dread the answers."

CHAPTER THIRTY-TWO

It was morning when they arrived at the Bunker. Their travels took them the long way in case of pursuit. After hours of back roads, Metcalf's car slipped beside the apple orchard behind the yellow farmhouse.

She opened the door, and the wind rushed against her. A shower was in the cards, as was an eight-hour stretch in bed. Yet, staring at the steel door barring them entry to their secret hideout, Metcalf felt both were far away.

Events played over in her mind. St. James would never have popped up on her radar without Nixon. He was a cereal mogul, not the kind of nefarious conspirator she'd imagined after dealing with Stallworth and Sullivan. Facing him brought the whole situation to another level. Their encounter made the fight more real than it had been for her—more real, and much more achievable.

The door shut behind her. Nixon tucked his coat tighter, still clutching his tablet in one hand. His eyes widened at the sight of the steel door. "You built a secret headquarters into a hillside? Awesome."

Metcalf smiled. "I'm glad someone finally said it."

She lifted the panel next to the door and entered her code. The metal groaned as it welcomed them home. Nixon was inside before they finished opening. There was a hop in his step that defied any level of exhaustion from the long night.

Before Metcalf could join him, Kanigher's hand fell on her arm. "Hold up a sec, would you?"

Metcalf turned to Nixon. She stepped inside the elevator and keyed the entry to her palm print. The doors began to shut, and she moved back outside.

"Don't break anything, Agent Jessup."

His lips curled. "I could get used to that."

The metal doors boomed shut. Metcalf stood before them, proud of bringing Nixon into the fold. To see him by their side, and enthusiastic at the job ahead, warmed her heart. The look from Kanigher, however, threatened to cool her down real quick.

"I'm not going to argue with you about this again," she said.

Kanigher shook his head. "Wasn't my plan either."

"But?"

"You called the cops on him, didn't you?" Kanigher asked. "I've spent the entire drive trying to figure it out, and that's all I keep coming back to. You brought heat down on Nixon to pressure him into accepting your offer."

"Bobby…"

"I get it, I do. We're up against the wall. Those guys with St. James? They were ex-military. Expensive talent for taking out a lone civilian."

"That's what I thought too," she admitted.

"That's what Nixon is, though," Kanigher continued. "He's not a field agent. He's not even Zac Modine, someone who went out for a job at the DSA to serve his country. Nixon is just a guy."

"Who we need," Metcalf said. "You have to see that now."

"I do," Kanigher replied. "I wish to God I didn't."

"That's not—"

"You manipulated him, Susan," he said. "You twisted the situation to your own ends to score the win. To get him here. There will never be a justification for that."

"You're right."

"Wait, what?"

Metcalf cleared her throat. "Don't make me repeat it, because I won't. My approach was heavy-handed. I saw an asset in Nixon, and I might have gone a little too far to bring him in."

"That's not the end of it, though, Susan."

"I know," Metcalf said. "I should have trusted in the team about recruiting Nixon. If I had, maybe we could have tried something different."

Kanigher huffed. "God forbid the truth doesn't work for a change."

"Can we take that chance?" Metcalf snapped. Her hand shot up before Kanigher could reply. "Sorry. Reflex. I'm still adjusting to this new dynamic, Bobby."

"So am I." Kanigher shifted closer. He reached out and took her by the hand. "I should have trusted your judgment more."

"You were right to question me. We're hiding here. True, we might not be on the run from the law any longer, but we're still ducking too many threats. And the cost? The cost has been way too high."

"I miss Jake too. Grissom was the best brother I ever served with. When he fell…" Kanigher went silent, his gaze down to the cold earth.

Metcalf shook her head. "When I lost him."

Grissom's betrayal continued to hang between them. It was another unspoken secret separating them, blurring the lines of trust and communication.

"That's the past." Kanigher lifted her gaze to meet his. "It has to be, or this won't work. It's time to build something new from the ashes. A new foundation for the DSA."

She liked the sound of that: a clean slate, and a better path forward. There was no more government oversight, no more outside influence over their mandate. They knew who the enemy was: the Trust. Now it was just a matter of putting names and faces to the threat to end their reign of terror.

"The Trust has us in numbers and resources," she said. The cold analytics of the situation returned. "What do we have?"

"Each other," Kanigher answered. "I know I'm not Grissom, but I'm here and I believe in the fight. Trust in us, Susan, and we will do the same."

"That simple?"

"Never," he said. "But it's a start."

The truth about Grissom threatened to fall from her lips. She swallowed the thought just as quickly. Knowing the truth about the man Kanigher called his brother might have been too much. It might have pulled him away from the mission ahead. She couldn't take a loss like that, not after everything else.

Instead, she buried the truth about Grissom with the rest of her secrets. It was better to be cautious with those around her. Secrets still had their place for Metcalf.

"Thank you, Bobby."

Kanigher nodded, then led them to the waiting lift. "How about a drink? To toast a new beginning."

Metcalf chuckled. She took him by the hand and headed inside. "I think that is the best offer I've had in a very long time."

CHAPTER THIRTY-THREE

Ben sat in the dim light of his room. He leaned against the footboard of his bed, his legs sprawled before him on the floor. Sleep was on the docket, yet refused to come to him.

Instead, his mind raced. The files offered by Wesley sat beside him, the first few open on his lap. They provided insight into the career of a man too brave or too stupid to quit asking questions.

Ben was proud to have met the man, and for the opportunity to carry on his legacy.

The DSA wasn't dead and buried. It merely evolved into something else now, something new and exciting. What that was remained a question mark to be sure, but the foundation was there — built brick-by-brick by those willing to stand up and continue the efforts of men like Wesley Fuller.

The casefiles fascinated him. Each one opened Ben's eyes to a new line of inquiry. He made connections to stories his father had shared with his mother during his youth, unaware of the young man listening in on each word. What they meant, what conclusions they brought up, remained a mystery, but one Ben was more than happy to pursue.

A knock at the door startled him. Before he could rise or respond to the abrupt interruption, the handle turned and the metal slab slipped loose from the frame. Morgan stepped in, fists balled up at her sides in a rage.

"I can't believe it!" Morgan slammed the door behind her. She paced across the room, not bothering to notice Ben at the base of his bed. "How could this happen?"

"Something bothering you, Morgan?" Ben asked, with a wry

smirk on his face. He enjoyed the passion she displayed. It reminded him he wasn't alone in their endless search for answers. He couldn't think of anyone else he would rather have at his side during this journey.

"What?" Morgan ended her pacing. "Of course, something is bothering me! Why isn't it bothering you?"

"Mostly because I don't know what we're talking about, but don't let that stop you."

Morgan sighed. She grabbed his desk chair, straddled the seat, and leaned forward along the back. "The body is gone."

"What body?" Ben asked. His eyes widened. "You mean the hunter guy?"

"We need a better name for that."

"I have some ideas, if that's what—"

Morgan threw him a thin glare. "Yes. The hunter guy."

"How?"

"He was in transit to the local morgue," Morgan said. "I made the arrangements to pick him up for further analysis. They just called to tell me he never arrived."

"They have any idea where he went?"

"Not a one," Morgan answered. She rubbed at tired eyes. "The wagon was stopped en route. According to the driver, military personnel claimed the body was a public health risk."

"Military personnel?" Ben ran the phrase over his tongue. He grew tired of dealing with men in uniform. "Anyone we know?"

Morgan nodded. "Orders came from General Adams' office."

The man from the Bellbrook incident. Ben nearly jumped out of his skin hearing the name. He knew Adams' involvement meant something more now, something they hadn't realized during their visit to the small town in Ohio.

"The Trust."

Morgan slammed her hands against the chair, then stood. "Dammit, Ben, you were right. The Trust is the mission. We should be doing everything we can to stop these bastards."

"Morgan..."

"Every time we don't, every time we turn our backs on them, they are there with a knife at our throats. What the hell could they even want with the body?"

Ben stayed silent. The answer frightened him. If the hunter truly came from the future, if people were being converted into monsters with the goal of tracking down enemies to those in power, then the reason the Trust wanted to study one was clear: to create their future weapon today.

"I should have listened to you, Ben," Morgan continued, not noticing his musings. "If I had—"

"Wesley might have been killed," Ben finished, cutting her off. "Wesley, and who knows how many others?"

"What are you saying?"

"That I was wrong," Ben said. "Now, I know that might be hard to believe."

"Not so hard," Morgan shot back. She sighed and leaned against the back of his door.

"You were right," Ben said, ignoring her immediate satisfaction. "The Trust isn't the only danger out there. People need us, need the DSA to do the job no one else will."

"You believe that?"

"If you do, I do," Ben said. "I'm not going to obsess about the Trust. But I sure as hell am going to bring them down when the time comes."

"And I'll be right there with you," Morgan said. She pushed from the door, then reached for the handle. "I shouldn't have just—"

"It's okay."

She pointed to the documents on his lap. "What are you looking through?"

"Wesley's casefiles," Ben replied. "He gave them to me. Thought they might be useful."

"Are they?"

"I'm not sure. Not yet, anyway."

Morgan nodded. She opened the door. "You should be resting."

"Five more minutes, *Mom*," Ben said. Morgan closed the door behind her and left him in the dim light once more.

Ben rubbed his eyes. He definitely needed to rest. The casework could wait one more day. He would probably need a week to get through everything, anyway.

As Ben stood, the files slid from his lap. Paperwork and photos scattered across the floor. He bent to retrieve them, and one image threatened to slip away. Ben snatched it, pulling the photo close for a better look.

In the image, Wesley wore a tan trench coat, his badge tucked in his front pocket. It was a picture from his earliest days in law enforcement. Something was cut off from the image, however. It had been folded to fit in a smaller frame by the looks of it. Ben moved for his desk and the lamplight. He opened the photo and spread it on his desk. His mouth stood agape at the second man in the photo.

Joshua Falk stood at the side of Wesley Fuller. Wes' partner stood taller and was shrouded in a black three-piece suit. He wore a fedora atop his head that matched his suit in color. None of that staggered Ben, not until he noticed the rounded spectacles hiding the man's eyes from view.

"It can't be."

CHAPTER THIRTY-FOUR

Wesley woke in his chair in the common room. The nap had been unexpected. He had never been one to sleep away the day. There was always something to do, something to see or question—be it the never-ending cycle of newscasts on the television or the inane drama from the other residents of the retirement home.

Not today. Wesley woke reinvigorated. The sun shone through the open window, blinding him for a moment to the world around him. There was no noise in the room, not the creaking of wheelchairs or the stamping of walkers through the corridors. In the emptiness of the room came a newfound peace for Wesley.

Everything was different. The nightmares of the past were forgotten, folded and tucked away, much like the files from his time at the DSA. All had been passed off to the next generation to carry on the fight. His struggle ended the second the monster fell.

He wasn't sure what to do next. He had been running for so long, life had passed him by. It was a new day, and he wasn't about to let it go without a fight.

Wesley vacated the chair. The cold suddenly returned once he left the sunshine behind and started for his room. Edna entered; a grimace formed the second she saw him. He didn't rise to the bait, and threw her an overzealous wave that nearly caused her to crash into the wall out of surprise.

"Have a splendid afternoon, Edna," Wesley said with a wink. "Television's all yours."

"What?" Edna asked in confusion. "But... Where are you going?"

"For a walk," Wesley answered. "Gorgeous day like this needs to be lived."

Wesley continued down the hall for his room and his coat. He snickered at Edna's mutterings as he left her behind. She would never change, and he couldn't say he wanted her to. His own change was necessary, the grumblings of a man too afraid to let go of the mistakes of the past. Those days were gone, though.

Now there was only the future to look toward.

One last piece of the past remained, though, linking Wesley to that terrible night in 1972. He waited in Wesley's room, black fedora and black suit in place despite the raging heat in the building. He cast a long shadow in the room, staring out the window and never looking back at the new arrival.

"Hello, old friend," said Joshua Falk, though most knew him by a different name now. For them, including those at the DSA, he was known as the Witness.

Wesley took one look at his friend from the doorway and smirked. "I was wondering when you would show up."

The man with the opaque glasses turned and smiled. "Too late, it seems."

Wesley fought back a laugh. He slipped into the room and closed the door behind him. "A joke from you? Things really are dire, then."

"They always have been." The man smiled at Wesley, extending a hand to his shoulder. "Though I am glad to see you in such good spirits, and in good health."

Wesley nodded. He didn't need to view the man's eyes to know he was hiding something. "That's not why you came, though, is it?"

The hand fell away. Slowly, the Witness made his way to the bookshelf in the room's corner, and the empty frame sitting prominently on display. A curious glance passed to his friend.

Wesley took his meaning immediately. "They needed to know what happened. About the case… and about you."

"I don't disagree." The man sighed. He returned the frame to the shelf.

"You wish you could, though, don't you?"

"The DSA would have learned the truth eventually," Falk

said. His smirk brought one to Wesley's face. "And you always loved to tell a good story."

"The monster is dead," Wesley said. He sat on the edge of his bed. "I did kill it, didn't I? It's finally over."

"In a way," the man replied. "In another, it's all just begun."

Wesley groaned. "Cut that crap out, Falk. I'm too old to deal with temporal mechanics. Or listen to you play your games. I need to hear it straight. Was I too late to make this right, old friend? Do we have any chance of stopping what you've seen from coming to pass? Can we save the future?"

Falk hesitated to answer, almost afraid to respond. When Wesley knew him back in the seventies, the man had never known an ounce of fear. As the silence hung between them, Wesley felt his chest clenching tighter. The old terror returned for an instant, then settled as his friend patted his wrinkled hand.

"There's still time, Wes." Falk returned to the window and the shining sun.

"Not as much as you would like," Wesley said.

"Never," Falk said. "Time is always the one enemy we cannot defeat."

"It's not just us anymore." Wesley joined him at the window, pulling at his old friend to face him, and the truth of what Wesley had seen these last few days. "Others have picked up the fight."

"I know." Falk fixed his hat, turning for the door.

"Then you know the time for secrets is over," Wesley called after him. The man known as the Witness stood in the doorway's darkness with his back to his friend. "The DSA deserves the truth, Falk. They need to hear it from you. Before everything falls apart."

ABOUT THE AUTHOR

Lou Paduano is the author of the Greystone series of urban fantasy adventures, which follow Detective Greg Loren and Soriya Greystone as they hunt myths, monsters, and legends in the city of Portents.

He is also the author of the conspiracy thriller series, The DSA, a serialized tale about a clandestine government agency trying to discover the true power behind humanity's future.

Lou lives with his wife and three daughters in Grand Island, NY. You can learn more about his books, including upcoming releases and free content by visiting his website at loupaduano.com.

THE GREYSTONE SAGA

AVAILABLE NOW

Follow the adventures of Soriya Greystone and
Detective Greg Loren as they hunt dangerous
myths and legends in the city of Portents.

BOOK ONE - SIGNS OF PORTENTS
BOOK TWO - TALES FROM PORTENTS
BOOK THREE - THE MEDUSA COIN
BOOK FOUR - PATHWAYS IN THE DARK
BOOK FIVE - A CIRCLE OF SHADOWS

GREYSTONE-IN-TRAINING

AVAILABLE NOW

For years, Soriya trained to become the Greystone.
Follow the trials that made her the protector
Portents needed to fend off the darkest of threats.

BOOK ONE - HAMMER AND ANVIL
BOOK TWO - THE GIFTS OF KALI
BOOK THREE - THE FINAL GAUNTLET

When the Trust systematically destroyed Ben Riley's life, there was collateral damage to those around him. Emily Wright has been missing for the last eight months, her entire existence erased. Now, after endless worry, a mysterious phone call from Emily has brought Ben to Wichita with Morgan Dunleavy in tow.

Their lead offers no answers until the pair meets Lizzy Doyle—a photojournalist with an obsession over the missing of the world. With this new and eccentric player comes a fresh case. A coed has been abducted, and the search is on.

Are the two cases connected? What secret does Lizzy bring with her about the missing? And when Ben chooses to follow this mysterious new companion over Morgan, will it spell the end of their partnership?